Be[(com)ing] REAL

A Coming-of-Age Story for Twenty-Somethings

by
Megan Noelle

Llumina Press

ISBN: 978-1-59526-657-6 (PB)
    978-1-59526-658-3 (HC)
    978-1-59526-659-0 (Ebook)

Printed in the United States of America by Llumina Press

Library of Congress Control Number: 2006909040

Foreword:

Coming-of-Age is a term that is often limited to the time in one's life when s/he transitions from a preteen to a young adult, where some innocence is lost, and some understanding of "how the world really is" is gained. However, this is not a process that occurs only once in one's lifetime. It is something that actually happens several times throughout it—each time that a new sense of *reality* is attained.

In the pages to follow, Kenny and Donna will explore their second coming-of-age: the time in their lives when they will transition from acting adults to actual adults.

Donna DiSimone

How did such a beautiful name get linked to such an ugly girl? Her name was not all that Donna had, but did not deserve. She had loving friends and family—people around her who insisted she was not the troll she knew was. She had always been embarrassed whenever someone referred to a beautiful woman as a donna, hating to be reminded of how she disgraced the name. She loved her name—that was not the issue—but she did not feel it was right for her. It was one positive attribute she had, though. Better to disgrace *Donna* than be stuck with something awful.

The first time Donna knew she was fat, she was four years old, sitting on the railing of a friend's deck, eating an ice cream (go figure), when she caught her reflection in the large window of the house twenty feet in front of her. She was wearing a swimsuit, and saw the folds of her stomach and realized what it meant. Her friend Paula was long and skinny enough that her swimsuit was baggy. Paula was eating a fruit Popsicle, her mouth stained cutely with it. Donna had a big chocolate dribble all down her front. Paula's blonde hair was pulled back in a pretty braid. Donna's was a messy brown bob she hated. She was ashamed, for the first time, of how she looked.

At age nineteen, Donna was five feet, three inches tall, and weighed over 170 pounds. Though clearly overweight, most people would not have identified her as especially "fat," and certainly not "obese," but in her eyes, she was disgusting, and all she could do to punish herself for it was eat more. *You like being fat? Here, get fatter,* she would say to herself in moments of retaliation.

If Donna had ever bothered to count, she would find that in her fifteen-minute walk from home to campus, she put herself down over forty times, frowning and feeling glum every time she caught a glimpse of her reflection. The worst moments were when she had had a particularly positive self-image for the day until she got a good look at herself in the mirror—finding an unknown roll protruding over her waistline, or that the hairstyle she had taken such care in arranging made her face appear four times chubbier than normal. It was enough to wreck any day.

Miraculously, by age twenty, Donna had finally had enough and spent a long summer dieting and exercising. It took only several months to shed over fifty pounds, but even after several years, she had not quite shed her *fat girl* self-image

1

Donna DiSimone was trying to decide if even after all she had done to transform herself into a less offensive being, she had ever come to deserve her name. Though she knew she could never match its grace, she also knew how much more insulting she could be toward it. Whatever she decided, her name would be abandoned in less than a year, and then perhaps her obsession with it would fade, as well. As she considered the matter, she gazed down at the engagement ring on the ring finger of her left hand, smiling to herself as she twisted it from side to side to watch the light sparkle off the stone.

The phone at her desk rang, startling her from her musings. Donna stopped daydreaming, transitioning into a businesslike tone as she spoke. "Donna DiSimone, how may I help you?"

"Well, you could start by—" began an exaggerated, suggestive voice, but Donna interrupted her dear friend Kenny the second she recognized the voice to be his.

"No way! Kenny!" Donna cried out, as though she had never expected to hear from him again.

"Well, someone's a little perky this morning," he commented, though his excitement mirrored hers.

"I'm so glad you called. For once in my life, I have news. I doubt I've ever had news before, and now I have the best news there is!"

Kenny was thrown. He had spent so much time steeling himself for what he was about to divulge that he had not even considered that Donna might steal the conversation from under him. "The best?" he asked nervously.

Donna was beaming on her side of the line, but when she heard his shaky comment, she thought perhaps she had been overzealous. "Oh," she said. "I didn't mean to go nuts. I suppose you did call me—"

1

Kenny was ashamed for dampening her spirits. That she could still read him so well reassured him, but after her ebullient intro, he did not know if he could proceed as planned. "No, no," he said, trying to sound as though she had not ruined his plans. "What's the news?"

Donna could not reclaim her enthusiasm when Kenny's tone was so dire. "Kenny, come on, what is it?"

Kenny sighed heavily. Donna could not quite tell if he was crying. She gave him time to relax, easing him along.

"I just don't—" he trailed off, running his free hand through his dark, wavy hair, sighing again, trying to remember the words he had recited.

"Don't what?" Donna led, growing concerned.

Kenny gave an odd laugh, as though he was a little embarrassed and ashamed of himself. After a long, drawn out sniff, he tried again. "Okay, so I thought this was gonna be easier on the phone." He paused, and Donna gave him his space without interruption. "I didn't mean to spoil your mood, but I wanted to talk to you about some things."

Thousands of possibilities were swimming in Donna's mind. She had no idea where Kenny had called her from, but wished she could appear there instantly to finish the conversation.

Kenny took her silence as an indication to continue. "You have always been incredibly supportive of anything I've done, or how I've acted. You're my best friend, and that's why it's so odd for me to tell you this. I don't want you to think I've been lying to you all along, or that I am lying to you now. I'm pretty confused, myself. I guess it's just that, not too long ago, something in me clicked. I lost the need to impress others, and I tried being me, for once."

Now *millions* of possibilities were swimming around in Donna's mind. She just kept listening, though, knowing that the point must be about to show itself.

"That's probably why I have been kinda standoffish these past months. I feel guilty for that, but I had to sort some stuff out for myself before I could tell anyone else about it."

Donna sank in her chair. She knew she ought to feel guilty as well. "Don't blame yourself for not keeping in touch, Kenny. I've been a little preoccupied, too." Donna twisted her ring again, nervously this time.

"Yeah, well, this has something to do with the person I've been dating for the last couple months," he admitted with difficulty.

Donna nodded, as though Kenny was right there in front of her.

"Her name is Tianna," Kenny threw out, and then stopped.

The thought now in Donna's mind weighed it down quite heavily. *Her* name. *Her* name is Tianna? Did this mean Kenny was with a drag queen, a cross-dresser—was he dating someone who was going to become a woman?

"What do you mean *her*?" Donna finally asked. "Is she some kind of performer?"

Kenny laughed a little, following Donna's thought. "No. She works at her father's art gallery."

Donna was completely baffled and a little irritated. "All right, Kenny. It's time to start filling in the blanks. I don't even know what to guess."

"I've been dating a girl," Kenny said plainly.

"A girl?" Donna sounded doubtful. "You mean like a cross-dresser?"

"No. I mean a female, not a she-male. A true, born-that-way, girl."

Donna was surprised, but was sure there had to be more. "That's it? That's the whole story?"

Kenny felt a little invalidated by her lack of outright disbelief.

"It?" he stressed.

"Well, damn, Kenny, you had me set up for the whole 'I'm becoming a woman' speech," she said, as though there was an outline for the topic. "I mean, yeah, I'm surprised! Hell, yeah, I'm surprised, but it's something I can handle." She lowered her voice a little, as a co-worker had peeked into her cube at her initial outburst.

Kenny's validation had finally come through. "Sorry, I guess I'm just afraid of how people are going to react. I mean, I've only told one other person, and that did not go so well. I mean, I think my dad will be just as indifferent as ever, but it's going to crush my mom," he admitted.

"Did you tell Marcos?" Donna asked sympathetically, knowing that Kenny's friend/boyfriend of several years probably would not have taken the news well.

"Yep," Kenny sighed. "He's the one I told." He sounded regretful, but proud. "I figured he deserved it most."

Donna agreed, but could not say she understood how difficult it was to go through, because truthfully, there was so much she never would understand. She caught a glimmer of her engagement ring out of the corner of her eye and gave a defeated laugh. How full of herself she had been. How insensitive of her it had been to just boast out her great news when Kenny was coming to her for empathy and support. She glanced at the counter on her phone.

Straightening, she cleared the emotion from her tone and spoke a little more professionally. "Kenny, I'm sorry, but we've already been talking for a while."

"I know," he laughed, sounding like he had just gotten over an intense crying spell. "I'm already ten minutes over on my break."

"We gotta hang out, though. I wanna see you in person and really talk this through, okay?"

Kenny nodded. Donna could not see it, though she somehow knew he had.

"You still have the same work e-mail?"

"Unfortunately." Kenny rolled his eyes, wishing he could have had some say in how his address had been formatted. "KennyG, that's me."

"All right, give me a minute, and I'll e-mail you a time and place to meet," Donna finalized.

"Will do," he said as they ended the connection.

Donna was more than a little frazzled by what she had learned, but was glad that Kenny had shared it with her. She had worried lately that they were drifting apart, but now she believed they needed each other more than ever. Plus, at least one thing had been settled: she would no longer have to worry about trying to fit a male bridesmaid into her wedding party.

Later that night, Kenny was already waiting for Donna when she arrived at the tea and coffee shop where they had agreed to meet. She noticed the lack of his usual stylish, though totally unnecessary, eyewear. He still had his fresh-faced good looks, fashionable attire, and well-coifed hair, but he had somehow morphed from chicly gay, to dashingly metro-sexual. It was so odd that Donna feared she was staring and quickly averted her eyes, wondering if her opinion of his appearance would have been the same had she not known about his recent change of lifestyle.

"Look at you, all shy," he commented, standing to greet her, as she approached the table.

Again, Donna got that less-gay vibe from him, his words the same as usual, but his tone more subdued. She allowed him to assist her with her coat and hang it over her chair before wrapping her arms around him and giving him a huge kiss on the cheek.

"Miss me?" Kenny asked, falsely doubtful.

"You know I did!" Donna answered, suddenly giddy for merely being back in his presence. "You abandoned the glasses? Not so studious now that you've left college?"

"Actually, Tianna doesn't like them—she thinks they make me look a little gay," he laughed, unable to help himself.

"They make you look extremely gay—wasn't that the point?"

Kenny raised his eyebrows and shrugged as though there was no defense, enjoying the joke. "Well, let me get you a drink. This place is kind of crowded, so I don't want us both to get up."

Donna sat back after placing her order with him, taking a moment to actualize his hetero-ness. She never knew there was a reserved gentleman under all that flair.

Kenny watched Donna's reaction to her first sip with amusement. "Don't you like it?"

"I can't tell," she replied, still contemplating the matter.

"You said that's what you always get here," he laughed awkwardly. "Did they make it funny?"

"No," she said plainly. "It's how it always is, I just don't know if I like it. I'm not really into tea. In fact, I generally hate it unless it's really sweet, lemony iced tea."

"Why don't you just get a vanilla latte with coffee then?" Kenny laughed, realizing how dearly he had missed her.

Donna shrugged. "I don't know. There's an element of it that's appealing." She tapped the fingers and thumb of her left hand, one at a time, as she thought. "But then there's something that makes me wanna—" she shuddered and wrinkled her lips with disgust.

Kenny was thoroughly entertained. "Suit yourself."

After a brief pause, Donna said excitedly, "So, tell me about Tianna."

Kenny looked around nervously at the sound of his girlfriend's name, as though he was afraid she was standing behind him, listening, and then silently apologized as he saw Donna's curious reaction.

"She is gorgeous," Kenny stated emphatically, as though picturing her.

Donna felt a little disappointed that the first thing he mentioned was her appearance, but kept it to herself.

"She's very Italian, her dad is a painter, and her brother is a chef, so all we talk about is food and wine and art." He glowed.

"You hang out with her family a lot, then?"

Kenny nodded. "Her brother makes the most amazing food—have you ever eaten at Loria?"

Donna shook her head. "I hear it gets great reviews, though."

Kenny agreed enthusiastically. "It's amazing; I should totally take you there some time. Anyway, their dad's gallery is adjacent to the restaurant. A lot of his work is displayed within."

Donna was in awe. "That sounds amazing."

"It is." Kenny, too, was taken by his own wonder. "And though Tianna is just this tiny little thing, I think she eats more than anyone, and she can put away a whole bottle of wine without ever seeming drunk."

Again, Donna felt uncomfortable. It was easy for a man to pick out any girl he wanted, the coveted ones always being effortlessly thin and beautiful, whereas she had to try hard every day just to keep herself looking on a level above *toad.*

"So, is Loria their last name?" she asked, trying to sound more interested.

Kenny nodded, taking a big drink through his straw. Donna hated it, but for the first time, she was starting to see Kenny as a regular guy, the kind that would ignore her, passing her up for some curly-haired blonde in a miniskirt, the kind that would have made fun of her to his friends a few years ago when she was heavier. She pushed her drink away, staring at the chocolate muffin an obese lady at another table was picking apart piece by piece, knowing she would look the same if she ate things like that again. Then there was Tianna, whom she imagined could eat a plate of spaghetti and meatballs the size of a trash barrel lid, and stay just as skinny as could be.

Food addiction is so unfair, she thought. *It's just as cumbersome an addiction as drugs, alcohol, or smoking, yet it is harder to quit because it cannot be completely cut from your life. Apart from needing it to survive, and having bodily cravings for certain nutrients,, most social events revolve around food. It's everywhere you look—TV commercials make your mouth water for it. Even if you can avoid a gluttonous sit-down meal, a drive down almost any street takes you past several drive-thrus and convenience stores, which are much more difficult to pass up.*

When Kenny's cup finally held nothing but ice, he put it down. "By the way, look at you," he said, as though he had only just set eyes upon her. "You look awesome, Donna. You're such a beautiful girl." He shook his head, as though he was looking at his own child, all grown up.

Donna felt spiteful, but smiled. She resented the comment, in truth—as though it had been born of obligation, rather than observation.

"I'll bet you can hardly fight off the boys these days." Kenny was being sincere, but he clearly did not understand how thoroughly he was offending Donna, as her inner response to his comment was, *You say, "these days," as though I wasn't formerly deserving of male attention, and now that I have lost weight, I somehow am? Though clearly, not as much so as your precious "Tianna," who is apparently not just cute and little, but artsy and cultured, as well.*

Kenny finally caught a whiff of her discomfort, and changed the subject. "So, what's going on with you? How's work?"

Donna glared at him outright. They had met to discuss *his* love life, and he had just assumed she did not have one of her own—that she might not like to reciprocate, like an equal. Or was she just that much of an abomination that the idea was too appalling to even fathom?

"Work sucks," she grumbled simply, not relenting on the glare.

"Donna, what the hell just happened?" Kenny asked, flummoxed.

"What?" she said, pretending everything was normal.

"Why the hell are you all pissed at me?"

"I'm not," she said in a small voice.

Kenny gave her one of his old "please, girl" looks of intolerance.

A laugh broke Donna's determined attitude, and she let it go. A little bit of something they once had came back to her. She apologized bashfully, not looking at him.

"That's better. Now, let's start again. What's going on with you?" he asked, as though he had already rehearsed it several times and was bored with the phrase.

Donna shrugged, but as her resentment faded, a gaiety began to take over. Slowly, she pulled her left hand out from under the table and flung it down in front of Kenny, not looking directly at him.

His jaw dropped as he lifted her hand to examine to the sparkling gem. "No, you didn't!" he exclaimed, though the words came out slowly and breathily.

Donna was beaming and blushing when their eyes finally met.

"So, I guess this was the news you referred to earlier?"

She nodded, unable to calm her smile.

"I suppose it's your turn to tell all, then," he prodded.

"Well, his name is Cameron. He used to be the trainer where I work, but he has since moved on to another company."

"Because of you?"

Donna was hesitant, and wound up shrugging as her answer. "So, he's really cute, and we hit it off once we started actually dating. He's a big dork, but he's kind, and treats me well, and puts up with all my moods—"

Kenny blushed just watching her speak of him. "I can't believe you won't be Donna DiSimone any more—that's really gonna mess with me."

"Donna Ellis isn't so bad," she said, though not with as much as enthusiasm as she could have.

Kenny decided not to linger, in case it was an uneasy subject. "Did you get to pick out the ring, or did you not know it was coming?"

"Actually, it has been in his family since his grandmother wore it."

"Wow!" Kenny looked closer. "It's so dainty—very you."

Donna took the compliment without bitterness.

"It was very romantic, and though I knew that it was inevitable, I did not know it was going to come when it did."

"This is so exciting! When did he ask?"

Donna went into a lengthier version of events, with Kenny enthralled by every detail. By the end, she wondered how she could have been so harsh earlier, and supposed that perhaps she had been a little jealous of Tianna at first. She had been the only girl in Kenny's life for so many years, and all of the sudden, he got this perfect little thing to replace her—though she now knew better than to think she would be replaced.

When it was over, Kenny congratulated her and offered to do all he could to help her with the wedding arrangements. She thanked him and said, "I can't wait for you to meet Cam. He's heard all about you, and I know you two are totally gonna hit it off. Well, not totally." Donna looked mischievous. "You don't see boys that way any more."

Kenny rolled his eyes at her, as though asking how long he was going to have to endure such comments.

"Well, it's crazy shit," Donna said to defend herself. "I mean, every time I think, 'Kenny's not gay,' I get this mental image of you in red Capri pants skipping to school with Marcos, and I wonder how in the hell it could be true."

Kenny looked bashful, but did not try to explain himself.

"Don't get me wrong, I don't disbelieve you, it's just that it will take a little getting used to before it sinks in completely, I think." Then, more seriously, she offered, "Do you wanna talk about how you came to realize—?"

Kenny shrugged, not looking very eager.

"We don't have to do it now, or at all, but the offer is on the table," she reassured him.

He nodded.

"So, when are the four of us getting together? If Loria's so great, why don't we all have dinner there some time?" Donna grinned, as though she knew Kenny was not quite ready to go that far yet.

"I hope you're toying with me." He half-smiled.

"She's never even heard my name, has she?"

Kenny wanted to melt, and felt he just might be doing it from the inside out.

"It is okay, Kenny. I understand the whole 'starting over' thing. It's hard to reincorporate some of the old things."

"You're not just some old thing," Kenny tried to explain, but Donna shook her head, not allowing it. "You take it as slowly as you need to."

Kenny could almost not believe the depth of her compassion.

"I know you haven't told your mom, because she would have called to yell at me for allowing it to happen, and that means you spend time with Tianna's family to avoid bringing her to yours, because of course, they would have no idea that you were even dating a girl." She wanted him to know that she truly did understand what was going on.

"I don't know why I even bothered to come here; you obviously already know anything I could tell you," Kenny laughed, amazed.

Donna giggled, too. "You're easy." She waved a hand at the wrist.

"Well, no, I haven't talked to my parents, and I haven't told Tianna the way things used to be. I don't really feel like things are that different." He shrugged. "I mean, I feel like the same old Kenny. It just seems to make sense to me why I never—" he hesitated. "With Marcos—I mean, if I was ever gonna be with a guy, wouldn't it have been Marcos?"

Donna shrugged as though to say she would have assumed so. "Well, have you been *with* Tianna?"

Kenny went rubicund. "Our attraction there was immediate."

"No way!" Donna could hardly believe it.

"What about you and *Cam?*" he asked in a lilted voice.

Donna looked guilty. "Well, I at least held out longer into the relationship than you did."

"It doesn't matter as long as you can't wear a white wedding dress," he teased.

She laughed sharply at the comment. "Hah! I earned that privilege fair and square, and though the whole thing might not be technical—it counts in my book—Cam is my one and only, even if it did start a little before the actual ceremony."

Kenny laughed again. He was enjoying himself so much that he had almost forgotten that he had agreed to meet Tianna at the gallery before closing.

"Aww," Donna whined.

"What?" Kenny tried to sound innocent.

"I saw you glance at your watch."

He sighed. "I'm sorry, but I promised Tianna to be at the gallery by nine. I'm barely gonna make it as it is."

"Okay," Donna pouted, looking down, but, she brightened almost immediately. "You'll have to tell her about me before too long, though. There's no way you're getting out of my wedding."

Kenny grinned. "You bet. I think I'll actually tell her tonight."

Donna and Kenny left each other feeling closer than they had been in many months.

When Donna went home to Cameron, they embraced and told each other how much each had missed the other, though they had only been apart two hours. Cameron already knew Donna had gotten the vanilla tea latte and had still not decided on it before she had even told him it had happened.

It was a different story when Kenny met with Tianna. He parked in front of the gallery, smiling as he watched her looking out the window, presumably for him. As he got closer, however, he saw that she was not smiling back and appeared to be glaring. She moved over to the door, Kenny able to watch her progress, as the entire front wall was of glass.

"You're late," was all she had to say, with ice-cold brass.

Kenny was a little taken aback by her abruptness. "Less than ten minutes," he said, looking down at his watch to make sure.

Tianna huffed and rolled her eyes. "It's a weekday, moron. We close at eight p.m. on weekdays and nine p.m. on weekends," she explained, as though to a simpleton. "Why didn't you check your voicemail anyway?" She did not allow an answer. "My brother is in the back, washing up. You'd better go tell him why he stayed so late waiting for you."

Kenny had the feeling in the pit of his stomach that he used to get as a teenager when he was afraid his parents had caught him for something big.

"Tianna, I'm sorry."

She turned and pointed him toward the back of the building, where the restaurant's kitchen was located.

Kenny was used to this kind of treatment from her, but it seemed to hit much harder after spending such a lovely evening with Donna. He was at fault, and would not have denied it, but at the same time, he had to wonder how Donna would have acted if it had been her there, waiting for Cameron. Somehow, he did not think she would have yelled at him—at least not before finding out why he was late. Kenny had the impression that Tianna could not have cared less whether he was hanging out with a friend, or in a traffic accident; if he had been late, she would have yelled at him. It made him wish he had been in an accident, just to see how she would react. Dejected, he marched off to find her brother Tony.

At least when Tony gave him a hard time, he was just playing. He even rolled his eyes at the fact that Tianna had yelled at him. "I don't know how you put up with her." He shrugged big, untying his apron. "I told her you probably just got the times mixed up." He made a gesture, as though to say it was no big deal. Tony sounded a bit thuggish, as he had adopted a hint of his father's tone and accent, but Kenny knew him to be good-natured. "Look, you gotta be careful with Italian women—they're either the sweetest little things you ever met, or they're the biggest pain-in-neck bitches. The problem is that most of them are both."

Kenny laughed, but he knew it was true, at least in Tianna's case.

"That's how they stay tough," Tony added.

Kenny nodded. Though he liked Tony very much, he was always shy around him.

Approaching a little closer than Kenny preferred, Tony said, "Look, I gotta get home. You just let Tia cool off for half an hour, and I swear the whole thing will be forgotten. By the time you get home, you guys will be onto some completely different topic." The clap on his back that followed was also a little harder than Kenny preferred.

Kenny loved the way Tony treated him. Even though he and Tianna had only been together for a couple months, he had never given him the 'big brother' routine. Tony had more respect for him than the other guys his little sister had dated because he was not totally into himself and never tried to boss her around. Kenny felt compelled to tell him about the way he had grown up and how he had never been with another woman, so did not quite know how to act sometimes. He knew it was the wrong time, however, and he was in no mood to be hated by Tony too, if he would have a problem with it. He had almost decided that perhaps Tianna was not the right girl for him—that perhaps he had been putting up with her attitude simply because he assumed all girls were like that. It had been made clear to him that evening, however, that girls like Donna were different—not that Donna was perfect; he was sure she had her own flaws, but Tianna was clearly not able to compare.

Kenny and Tianna did not speak one word to each other on the drive home or that night getting into bed together at his apartment.

The next morning, when Kenny stumbled into the dining area and took a seat by Tianna, who was already drinking coffee and reading the newspaper, he still felt uncertain about their relationship continuing.

She did not even look up to greet him as she stated, "We don't really have anything for breakfast, and I just used the last coffee filter for one of my flavored blends." She was clearly more interested in her article than in her boyfriend.

Kenny registered what she said, but made no response. He stared at nothing, thinking so hard he could not put language to his thoughts. After a bit, Tianna finally said, without removing her eyes from the article, "So, what made you so late last night? Were you lazing around playing video games, or did you go out and do something for a change?"

Kenny knew it was not supposed to be part of his new image, but she made him feel so awful that he wanted to run crying to his room and call Donna. He knew if he spoke, it would happen, so he tried to calm down, not looking at Tianna, afraid that if she caught his eyes, the urge would be even worse.

After a moment of silence, she looked up at him. A moment later, she finally put the paper down. "Kenny, what were you doing?" At last, there was some heat in her tone, though she was so curious, it was only a hint. "Why do you look ashamed of yourself?" The way she eyed him pushed him nearly to bursting.

"I'm not ashamed," Kenny said, but his voice was tiny and his head was bowed.

"Then why are you acting it?" she demanded, losing patience.

Kenny took a deep breath, but did not look at her as he spoke. "I'm not ashamed of anything. I'm upset because of the way you're treating me." He could not believe he got it out without his voice cracking.

"The way I'm treating you?" she shot back indignantly. "You showed up an hour late yesterday—no explanation, no 'let me make it up to you,' and now you sit here and won't say a damn word, and I'm treating you bad?"

"Forget it," Kenny said. "Wanna go get breakfast?"

Tianna sighed. "I guess," she said, but it was clear that though she could go for a bite to eat, she did not care to go with him.

They drove to a diner, never speaking a word at home, in the car coming or going, or at the table in the restaurant. By the time breakfast was over, he had still not told her about Donna, though the topic was crawling under his skin to get out. If for no other reason than to be able to communicate with Donna in the open, Kenny knew he could not delay the girls' meeting any longer.

"So, I got some great news," he finally piped up as they reentered the apartment and hung their coats in the closet near the front door.

"What's that?" Tianna asked, seemingly uninterested.

"One of my best friends is getting married," he beamed, focusing on keeping merry.

"Hmm," Tianna commented, as though he had told her the time.

Kenny saw that he would have to carry the conversation, and he did so bravely, if hesitantly. "She and I were best friends growing up; last night we went to coffee so she could tell me, and that's why I was late."

Tianna's interest did pique a bit at this. "*She* was your best friend? Why haven't you mentioned her before?"

Kenny shrugged. "I don't know, I guess because we haven't kept in touch so much since the year or two after college."

Her forehead wrinkled as though she was straining to recall something. "Oh, wait; is this that fat girl in all your pictures?"

The words slashed at Kenny's heart as he listened to Tianna laugh.

"Donna might have been a little heavy," he admitted with difficulty.

"Might have been?" Tianna scoffed. "I'm just thankful you two never took photos at the pool."

Kenny barely stopped himself from shouting aloud, *God! Why are you such a bitch?*

One good thing that came out of the conversation, however, was that Tianna saw no reason to fear him getting friendly with an ugly, fat girl, so she did not mind if Kenny talked to Donna or hung out with her. He did not bother to update her on Donna's physical appearance, a bit of mischief brewing, waiting to see Tianna's reaction when they finally met in person.

G rowing up, Donna was a grazer. She ate small amounts at a time, but she ate so often that it eventually added up into pounds and inches.

Kenny often ate as much as she did, but nothing was ever going to make that boy fat. Sometimes, Donna could have just killed him for it.

***

Kenny knocked on Donna's front door before letting himself in. He and Donna never minded each other's pop-ins. Sometimes her roommates had found them less than amusing, though not as awful as their Mariah Carey-screeching-neighbor at nine in the morning on weekends, as their room shared a wall with Kenny's boyfriend's bedroom the next apartment over. They often considered swapping rooms with Donna, though hers was half the size of theirs, because she should have to deal with it; Kenny was her best friend, not theirs.

"Hey, Kenny," Nikki said as she sleepily entered the kitchen in her Paul Frank pajamas.

Kenny acknowledged her with a wave and a smile. He sat down on the couch and waited for Donna, anxiously tapping his foot against the floor.

When Nikki joined him on the sofa with her bowl of strawberry cereal, she turned on the TV and began watching The Golden Girls.

"Damn! We missed the theme song," Kenny said disappointedly, as he leaned in excitedly. "I love this episode, though. It's when Rose is dating a little person, and Blanche thinks it's a practical joke, then she trips all over her words when she realizes that it's not."

Nikki agreed it was one of her favorites, as well. "Don't you think this show is a little marriage-proposal and

17

wedding-happy? It seems that one of the girls or someone they know, is always getting married, or considering marriage—"

Kenny agreed whole-heartedly. "And don't you think it's funny how so many of the weddings or attempted weddings take place at the house? I mean, can you imagine actually having a small wedding at your house every six months to a year?" Kenny laughed, tempted to ditch class just to finish the show.

Donna had still not come out of her room when he checked his watch a few minutes later.

"Doesn't she know what time it is?" Kenny whined. "I better go make sure she's up. I'm gonna be pissed if she's dead asleep."

Kenny walked the few feet to Donna's bedroom. The door was closed, so he knocked and waited. She muttered something he could not understand.

"Girl, get up and let me in, or I'm coming in," he warned.

Donna made another sound that was clearly an utterance of defiance and did not move to open the door.

Still minding Donna's privacy, Kenny pushed the door open slowly, calling to her. "Donna? What are you doing in there?"

Donna sniffled audibly. It was clear that she was going to break down crying at any minute.

Kenny maneuvered through the crack in the doorway; the door had caught on a stack of clothes, and would only open a quarter of the way. "Donna?" He sounded sympathetic, ready to comfort her.

When he came upon her, she was sitting on the floor before her closet, still in pajamas. Her face was in her hands, and she had obviously been crying.

"What's up, honey?" he asked her lovingly.

"I can't fit into any of my pants, that's what," Donna sassed. She was devastated, looking up at him with the saddest eyes he had ever seen on her.

Kenny sighed heavily. He crouched down and crawled over to her, opening his arms when he got close enough to hug her. Tightly embracing her, he made comforting sounds as he rocked her a little.

Donna felt she did not deserve his sympathy. "I'm so disgusting! Why do you bother?"

"Hey," Kenny said sharply, making her face him. "You know how I feel about that. Don't you ever say you're disgusting."

Donna stared at him, tears spilling down her cheeks. "I wish I could just wear a giant box so no one would have to see my figure."

"All right. That's enough of that. I'm gonna pick out something for you to wear," Kenny insisted, popping up, standing.

Donna's head flopped back down in her hands. "There's nothing in there I can wear," she whined.

"We'll just see," Kenny said optimistically, moving from item to item, sliding the hangers across the bar. "Where're your favorite jeans?"

"They're over there." Donna indicated them with her head. "I can't wear those any more. I've totally outgrown size fourteen. I'm gonna have to buy all sixteens, which means I'll have to shop at fat stores." She began crying all over again.

"Don't you have mostly boys' jeans anyway?" he asked. "I know you buy them oversized, so they should still fit."

"Yeah, but they're tight. They're supposed to rest on my hips, but they don't anymore. I just can't wear 38's. I can't," she sniffled.

Kenny decided it was time to stop asking about jeans. He looked on her closet shelf and found a pair of jogging pants. "These are totally cute," he said, holding them up trying to make them appeal to her. "What about these?"

Donna seemed to consider them. "Maybe," she conceded, "but I don't have a shirt I can wear with them. All my T-shirts are too small."

Kenny knew that was untrue. "I bet you have at least one." He searched. "How about this?"

He could tell by looking at her that the crying was about to start again. "I can't wear white—I'll look a big blob-banner for The Specials."

Kenny was getting irritated. He wanted to sympathize with her, but she was being impossible. "Okay," he said, putting the shirt back. He passed several more shirts until he got to a plain black one with a tiny Adidas logo on the breast. "This one's perfect. It's dark, it's plain, and I know it's not tight on you." He thrust the pants and shirt at her. "Now put this on and I'll turn my back to you," he ordered.

Donna began laughing at last.

"What?" Kenny demanded, spinning around, hands on his hips, causing Donna to laugh even harder.

"What are you handing me—clothes or a condom?" She burst out laughing.

From someone else, the joke might have been offensive, but from Donna, Kenny could laugh at it, too. "Just shut up, and put the damn outfit on. We've already lost too much time to stop at the coffee cart on the way," he snipped.

"It's okay. I need to lose a few pounds, anyway."

Kenny gave her a look, though he was still facing the wall. "It's just all about you today, isn't it?"

Donna smiled big and nodded merrily.

She could not help it. She was finally in a better mood. Kenny had actually picked out a decent outfit and she did not feel too "obvious" in it; "obvious" being a term Donna had coined to describe when she felt like she stood out for some reason—her outfit did not look right, did not fit right, or she had on clothes that were too bright or too funky. She wanted to attract as little attention to herself as possible, and when she felt she attracted too much, she felt conspicuous, or "obvious."

They walked to campus together, arms linked, talking in ebullient tones all the way. Kenny let Donna go at the building of her first class and went on to one about a hundred feet away for his, just slightly guilty, but glad to be apart from her for a couple hours. Though Donna often complained about her weight, that morning had been particularly trying.

2

Things with Tianna seemed to improve over the next few weeks, now that Kenny had Donna to confide in again. He had even been over and met Cameron several times, and the three of them got along like they had all been old friends. Donna, however, was afraid of the deep sadness he clandestinely exuded every time he spoke of Tianna. She thought he was only staying with her because he did not know what else to do—if things not working with her meant things would not work with girls in general. She, of course, knew this was untrue, but did not know how to convey it to him without expressing her doubts about Tianna, especially as she had not even met her or seen them interact with each other yet.

That was, perhaps, why Donna was so eager to assent when Kenny finally invited Cameron and her to have lunch at Loria one Saturday afternoon.

From the moment the girls were introduced, Donna felt about Tianna precisely as she had felt upon tasting the vanilla tea latte. She planned to keep an open mind while considering her, but if the deliberation of the latte was at all telling, the forecast was grim.

Tianna had to do everything in her power to keep her jaw from dropping to the pavement at her first sight of Donna. There was no way she could be the same girl in the photos. Her astonishment was completely unflattering, however sincerely she attempted to play it off, though Donna read it accurately and accepted it with delight. The guys, meanwhile, shook hands and smiled.

The lunch was not too awkward, helped greatly by Tony's antics when he came out to introduce himself and watch them taste the variety of appetizers he had sent out to them. Donna saw how Kenny could appreciate the atmosphere so much.

"So if we have met the chef, where's the artist?" Donna asked of the eldest Mr. Loria, whose absence was a bit disappointing, as upon perusing his various works, she would have loved to ask him some questions.

"You do not think my caprese is art?" Tony asked in a terrible, pained, French accent, making a plea to her on bended knee.

Donna could not keep from laughing. Even the boys joined in, though Tianna only gave a stiff grin and a heavy puff out of her nose, which might more truthfully have demonstrated indignation and annoyance rather than amusement. "Go find Dad," she ordered, sounding bored.

Under different circumstances, Donna might have been embarrassed by Tianna's tone; however, she was so over any attempt to impress or be impressed that her hostess' tone added to her enjoyment rather than detracted from it.

It was the defining moment in which Donna decided that Tianna was a "no go," and she needed to be honest with Kenny about it. Originally, she had planned that if she decided she did not really like Tianna, she would allow Kenny time to decide for himself what to do with their relationship. However, knowing how she had treated him, and seeing her complete lack of 'fun,' Donna decided to kick Kenny in the pants, nudging him to leave while it was still early.

The next day, Kenny went to Donna and Cameron's place to hang out, without Tianna.

"I know you hated her," Kenny announced as he entered their front door. He went immediately to the couch and flopped down, huffing.

"Hi, Kenny," she said lightly, sitting on the arm of the couch, leaning on him in a playful way.

Kenny frowned. "She really is an awful bitch, isn't she? I don't know why I keep thinking there will be some kind of change when she decides to drop the cold front."

23

"I hate to say it, Kenny, but I don't know if it's a front. I think, if nothing else, you can at least count on her to show you how she honestly feels," Donna said soothingly.

She thought Kenny might start crying, and it broke her heart to watch him struggle to stay stoic.

Kenny groaned, deeply frustrated with not just the situation, but with his whole life. "I just can't get anything right. I can't make it work with a guy. I can't make it work with a girl. What am I?"

"Kenny, this is just one girl. There are countless more out there just like her, but there are also a few here and there that are not. You just have to meet a few and find out what you like. Just because one relationship goes bad does not mean they all will—and it's stupid to stay in it if you know it's not right."

"But you found Cameron on your first try," he whined.

"I did," Donna admitted. "But though I never actually dated anyone else, I was always sifting through features and gathering thoughts and feelings about other guys. Plus, I'm a big weirdo who was always so involved with hating myself that I never really worried about liking someone else." She shrugged.

Kenny wondered if that was supposed to make him feel better. If anything, he seemed even more diminished.

"And if you're thinking of Marcos—"

Kenny looked up suddenly, as though she had accused him of something.

"Write him a letter or something."

Kenny's immediate reaction to that suggestion was that it was dumb and useless.

Donna shrugged. "I don't know, Kenny. I want you to get over this and move on. So you had a few bad dates, and I will have to sacrifice ever again having the best eggplant I have ever tasted, but that's all it is. It's nothing to be miserable about. Honestly, it's probably good for Tianna, too, because she can't possibly be happy either."

Kenny was slightly affronted by the suggestion, but he knew it must be true. Maybe by the time he wandered home, he would see it the same way. All he wanted to do now, though, was set it all aside.

"Plus, after a couple of years, they probably will have forgotten all about us, and we can go back to Loria for the food," she teased.

Kenny refused to cheer up. "Do you have stuff to make Bloody Marys?" he asked, peering up at her with his sweet doe eyes.

A huge grin came over Donna's face. "Of course," she practically sang. "Let's send Cam out for some giant olives and a pizza—what do you say?"

Kenny looked like he wanted to say yes, but thought it was rude. Donna waved the implication away, calling, "Ca-am!"

Smiling, Kenny added, "You'll have to get some more vodka, too."

"We have, like, half a bottle."

"I plan on being here a while."

Donna laughed. She had 'old Kenny' back for a day, at least, she knew.

So much for the kick in the pants, Donna thought upon learning a week later that Kenny and Tianna were still an item. Tianna had been so taken aback by Kenny's attempt to dump her that she agreed to shape up if he stayed with her. Apparently, she really did like Kenny, and at least according to what Donna had heard, she just had not known how to show her feelings. She usually dated guys that fled if they felt her getting too attached, so she tried to keep Kenny as distant as possible, so he would stick around. Donna still did not trust her as far as she could throw her, but then again, she had just started doing ten to twenty push-ups against the sink every time she went to the bathroom.

Cameron could not handle the drama, either, and rolled his eyes every time Donna filled him in on new events. By the time Kenny and Tianna had been dating three months, however, Donna found herself coming around to the idea that the girl she had once presumed was a worthless bitch might deserve a second consideration. That said, she went and had a vanilla tea latte with Cameron one evening after work. She left the shop still uncertain.

That same evening, Kenny was watching TV in his living room when Tianna came in, distracted by going through the mail. Furtively setting the stack on the bar near the entry, she concentrated on a particular piece, which she found of interest. In big, red letters, "RTS DECEASED" was printed across the front of the envelope. Kenny was the sender, and it was addressed to Marcos Cano—someone Tianna had never heard of. She did not bother to ask, but went ahead and opened the envelope. As she withdrew the card, a slip of paper fluttered to the ground. She let it sit on the floor while reading the card. It was of the "I miss you" variety and was signed, "Love, Kenny." Something about it seemed a little off, but she felt terrible telling him that whomever he had cared enough about to send the card to had died. She picked up the slip of paper and began to read. Her face went through an odd assortment of expressions as she did, comprehension dawning and fading intermittently.

I never wasted a tear on you,
I never squandered a dream.

Though I cried every day for you,
And dreamt every night between.

I never wasted a dime on you,
I never frittered an hour.

Though every day long I worked for you
With determination dour.

Never these things did you thank me for,
And never a time did I vent.

For, if ever I shed a tear, spent a dime, an hour, or dreamt,
It was always for you, always in love, and always was well-
spent.

She stood frozen for a moment before uttering a shriek of shock. Kenny turned to her upon hearing it.

"What... the fuck... is... this...?" she said in several slow and shallow breaths.

Kenny was caught unawares. "What?" he asked, unable to imagine what could have caused her reaction.

"Marcos Cano?" she demanded.

Before the name was even all the way out, Kenny had leaped off the couch, but then clenched up, as if he expected to be cracked over the head with a baseball bat, upon receiving her stare.

In his reaction, Tianna saw that her worst fear was true. "A love poem? To a guy?" she screamed, looking at him as if he were dog crap covered in ants.

Kenny made a few attempts at words, but failed. How she found out about it was not even on his mind, as he had written the message two months earlier and all but forgotten about it.

"You disgusting faggot! How could you touch me after fucking some guy? I don't even know how many guys you fucked!" It appeared she might very well throw up at the idea of it.

"I didn't—" Kenny tried to protest. His voice came out small and meek, and he could not hold back the paroxysm of emotion or the torrent of tears.

Tianna threw the letter to the ground and stamped on it. "Your disgusting faggot poem for your disgusting faggot boyfriend!" she cried. "Well, now he's dead, and I want to die, too! Maybe you gave me AIDS, and I will! I hate you! Burn anything of mine that is left here!"

She walked out, slamming the door behind her.

Kenny lay in a desperate heap on the floor. He stayed there, bawling uncontrollably for what seemed like hours. His whole world was destroyed: Marcos was dead.

When Kenny finally did drag himself from the floor, he stopped to pick up the pieces of the card. He saw the DECEASED stamp, and the poem written in his own hand that he had sent to Marcos months earlier to convince him that even though he no longer had romantic interest in him, he still loved him, and that all they had once had was not a lie. He held it to his heart as he stomped weakly to his room, got into his bed, and closed his eyes for a long, long sleep.

A couple of nights later, in bed before going to sleep…

"Damn," Donna exclaimed, more with dismayed acceptance than conviction.

"What?" Cameron asked, setting his book flat against his chest and turning toward her, a bit surprised, as he had assumed her asleep already.

"No more eggplant parmesan." Donna sounded like a child resigned to the fact that her favorite toy was damaged beyond repair.

"What?" Cameron half-laughed.

She, who had been facing away from him, turned over. "Kenny hasn't called me back. He and Tianna broke up."

Cameron thought she was being hasty. "You guys used to go months without talking—"

"I know," said Donna sadly. "This is different, though." She sighed. "I'm really worried about him. He always returns my messages—and the last one I left was two days ago. I should go see him." She rolled back to the side she had been on and sighed again.

Cameron did not know how to comfort her. He watched her for a moment, hating that she was sad. Eventually, he went back to his book with a defeated expression on his face.

A long moment later, sounding very sleepy and depressed, Donna muttered, "I don't like the vanilla tea latte, and I don't think I'll have one again."

D onna was sitting on the top step of the staircase just outside her front door, having a cigarette with Nikki, when Kenny and Marcos came bounding merrily up the stairs.

"What's so great?" Donna asked, sounding miserable.

"We're going camping!" Kenny shouted.

"What? You've never even been camping," she said, thinking it was nothing that would interest him.

"My family goes all the time," Marcos told her, as though to impress upon her that he knew how to take care of himself in the woods. "Well, we did as kids, anyway." He glossed over a hurtful emotion that had risen within him.

"It'll be fun. Paul, Mark, and Joaquin are all coming. You guys should come too, and Nikki, your sister, if she wants to," Kenny tried to entice them.

"Joaquin?" Nikki asked, jerking her head back as though she could not believe they actually knew someone named Joaquin.

"That's not his real name," Donna enlightened her grumpily.

"Yeah," Marcos took the floor. "We just call him that because he looks like Joaquin Phoenix." A kooky smile of delight crossed his features as he pronounced the actor's name. "Gladiator." He sighed with adulation, hands against his heart.

Kenny smacked him playfully on the chest. "What do you say, though, wanna come?" he asked Donna.

"I think it sounds like a boys-only party," she commented, looking to Nikki for agreement.

Nikki nodded.

"Oh, come on," whined Marcos. "It's not just fags in bags—anyone can come—except lesbians," he teased, making a face.

"I still think we'll pass," Donna reaffirmed.

29

"Okay, suit yourself," Marcos sassed and nodded to Kenny to follow him inside.

"Come by later," Kenny said, reaching a hand out to grasp the one Marcos held out to him.

3

K enny was indeed worth worrying about in the days after he received word of Marcos' passing. Between thoughts of wanting to join his friend in death, another kept resurfacing—a biting, feasting need for proof. He needed to see Marcos' apartment. He needed to see for himself that Marcos was not there, not sleeping, not watching TV, not having company. The last time Kenny had talked to him, Marcos had sounded down and impatient. Maybe he had not told Kenny he was dying because Kenny had been so into explaining his life choices—the embodiment of which had just stormed out without a modicum of compassion. Maybe Kenny had killed him. Maybe he had annoyed him to death, but how could he have known it was to be their last conversation? How could it have been the last— Marcos was a twenty-four-year-old boy. Everyone liked him, and Kenny simply adored him—adored everything about him, essentially became just like him—until it had become so clear that he was not.

He just had to see. That was it.

Kenny picked up the phone in his kitchen, noticing that everything looked exactly the same as it had when Tianna left, realizing that he had not been in it himself since then.

Donna's answer came quick, as though she had already had the phone in her hand. "It's about damn time!"

"Sorry." Kenny sounded bashful, but not nearly as gloomy as he had expected to sound.

"So, no more eggplant?" Donna asked knowledgably.

"Nope." Kenny shook his head as he sighed. "No eggplant and no Marcos."

"What?" Donna was unnerved by the bleakness in Kenny's tone. She had had no prescience of anything to do with Marcos, and the way Kenny's voice sounded when he pronounced his name…

Kenny gulped. "Marcos is gone, Donna. He's dead."

Donna could not process the information in an intelligible manner.

"Do you remember advising me to write him right after you first met Bitch? Well, I did, and the other day, the letter came back 'Return to Sender: Deceased.'"

Donna's hand met her mouth as she gasped. "My God," she breathed.

There was a long, silent moment.

"It's what caused our break-up," Kenny began again, speaking of Tianna. "She opened the card, and it wasn't really a normal card for two guys to exchange, but then she read the poem, and—"

"Oh, you wrote him a poem?" Donna simpered. She and Kenny had taken a creative writing class in high school, and Donna had always loved Kenny's poems, though she struggled to write them herself.

"Yeah," he said, reflecting how it had been his defeat. "I'm going to Tucson. I want to verify the news, and then maybe I'll be able to settle my grief."

"Are you sure you should drive alone?"

"Yeah. I think I got the worst of it out. It would be hell for you anyway—putting up with me the whole time. Plus, I don't know how long I am staying, if I am staying—"

"You?" she sputtered indignantly. "I just want to go to Tucson to eat. I think four nights, five days—nine meals—"

"I'd bring you back an Eegee's, but it would never make it in the heat," Kenny smiled.

"Well, call me if you change your mind, and if you need to talk, and if you're staying—I want to know."

"Thanks, Mom." Kenny sounded a little brighter.

"Well, it won't be too far off, now that I am getting married." She smiled hopefully.

Kenny raised an eyebrow. "Really?"

"We'll see."

"Well, I'm gonna get ready, then head out. If you happen to run into Tianna anywhere, kill her, will you?"

"I shall make my very best endeavor," Donna pledged cheerfully.

After they hung up, Donna thought that though it was the most dreadful distraction, at least the news had sobered Kenny up a little to Tianna's true nature.

Kenny pulled into the dusty parking lot of Marcos's apartment complex. He would always remember Tucson for the dust. There was an ominous feeling about the place, enhanced by the overcast sky. He was further daunted to see that Marcos' front door was propped open. He double-checked the apartment number, and it was definitely the right place. He suddenly realized that if Marcos no longer lived there, it was, after all, an apartment, and someone was likely living there. The thought was a bit sickening that Marcos could be replaced just like that, but then, Kenny did not even know how long Marcos had been dead. It appeared as though someone was moving in, so perhaps it was only now being rented again.

Still, Kenny approached. Looking around at the broad expanse of the complex, he noticed a moving truck with its ramp down. A moment later, a man came running down it—a man that could have been...

"Marcos?" Kenny asked aloud, knowing it could not be, even though it seemed it was.

The man turned toward Kenny, as though he had heard him, but he was much too far away for it to be possible. A surprised, but welcome look of recognition took him over, and he made his way jovially over to Kenny. Kenny was ecstatic for an ephemeral moment—but no. It was not Marcos. It was Felix, Marcos's older brother. His signature shoulder-length hair was pulled into a sleek ponytail at the base of his neck, moustache neatly tapered along his upper lip. Finally, something was familiar.

Kenny walked toward Felix recognizing him, and the two men embraced upon meeting.

"Hey, man. I can't believe you are here. I tried to locate you, but there was nothing in Marcos' things that had your contact info on it," Felix said as they broke apart.

"It's okay. I still found out," Kenny said sadly, though seeing Felix had raised his spirits.

"Well, our dad and I are taking his things home. We are going to sell and donate most of it, but you are welcome to take anything sentimental."

Kenny thanked him for the offer, but he was a bit on edge knowing that Mr. Cano was there, too. Marcos' father had never accepted his son's sexuality, and had kicked him out when he refused to deny it any longer. Marcos had gone down a horrible, destructive path, of which Kenny had only ever heard bits and pieces.

Felix seemed to know what Kenny was thinking. "It's okay. Dad and Marcos made up before he died. Dad is full of shame for what happened; he blames himself for the way Marcos died."

Kenny only then realized that he had never wondered how Marcos died; the fact that it had happened at all had been enough up to that point.

"You don't know," Felix said knowingly, stroking his moustache. "Marcos had AIDS, Kenny. He had known he had HIV for a long time, but never told anyone until he became very sick."

Kenny's insides caved in upon themselves. He felt as though his whole body was sucked into his bellybutton. He grabbed onto Felix for support. All he could think, seconds later, was, 'That bitch! That hurtful, awful—' as he remembered what Tianna had said before leaving.

"That's why I tried so hard to get in touch with you. I thought you needed to know. Marcos insisted that you were safe, but well, I just—"

Then something clicked for Kenny. That was why Marcos never pressured him to have sex—because he knew. It was why

Marcos could be so in love with him, but only seek his companionship. Kenny would never push the sexual angle because, while he did adore Marcos, it was more of a friendly admiration. That was why they worked. Still, Kenny felt Marcos should have at least told him. They had kissed, sometimes rather heavily, but every time, one of them had stopped it from going too far.

"Has there been a service yet?" Kenny finally gathered himself to ask.

Shame-faced, Felix nodded. "It was a few weeks ago."

Kenny felt himself about to cry. He was so mad! So unbelievably mad! Mad that he missed the funeral, mad that Marcos had not confided in him, mad that his father had kicked Marcos out and driven him into the life that caused him to contract HIV in the first place—just mad!

He felt himself grinding his teeth and stopped it.

"Kenny, I am so sorry that you had to find out like this." Felix looked like he might cry, too.

Kenny scanned the parking lot for George Cano, Felix and Marcos' father. He did not know how, but he wanted to exact his rage upon him.

"Kenny, chill out, man," said Felix, pushing against Kenny's chest to keep him in place. "I told you, Marcos and Dad made up. He did not die with a grudge, so don't you start one now. It's not worth it."

Over by the truck, George watched the younger men interact. When he gathered how Kenny felt toward him, he hung his head and cried into his hands. The guilt in his heart was hard enough to bear without the blame of others.

Kenny took a deep breath and calmed down at the sight. He looked at Felix and dropped his resistance.

"Easy now," Felix guided, lowering his hand.

Kenny shook his head as his face went soft, wanting to cry. "God, this just sucks!" Kenny pounded his fist on the pavement, seating himself in a whirl upon it. Felix put an arm around him and sat down, too. He whistled and motioned for George to join them. George was disinclined at first, but when Felix gestured, as though to say, 'Come on, damn it,' he came somberly, head bowed. The three men sat and grieved for a long few minutes before anyone spoke.

Clearing his throat, Kenny piped up, "Can I give you guys a hand with the truck?" Tears came now, even though it was most stable he had felt since first talking to Felix.

"I'd like that," George admitted, though he knew he deserved nothing but loathing, certainly not forgiveness and acceptance from the boy he had cursed with his own tongue upon seeing Marcos with him in the past.

The sadness in George's eyes was almost too much to bear. "Hey, at least *I* got to know him," Kenny said, smiling. "I can forgive you because I see your regret, which can never be mended."

George nodded, tears leaking from his eyes as though they would not stop for hours.

Felix got to his feet. "I'm gonna finish up the living room."

Kenny only vaguely heard the words, but when Felix began to walk away, he scooted closer to George and took his hand in his own, smiling at him as best he could manage.

Donna listened eagerly to Kenny's story when he got back from Tucson. (Not only did Donna no longer attempt to like vanilla tea lattes, but they had also abandoned the whole "tea and coffee" thing and gone back to just coffee).

"So, all in all, it was pretty peaceful," Kenny summed up, after Donna ordered her second decaf, non-fat, sugar-free syrup, vanilla latte.

Donna caught him smiling as she placed her order, and responded, "Hey, I have a wedding dress to get into eventually. It's bad enough they run, like, two sizes bigger than regular clothes' size, but I refuse to pudge out of it anywhere."

Kenny rolled his eyes. He did not think Donna would "pudge out" of anything, but knew if he commented, she would retaliate with some complicated explanation of all she does to find clothes that flatter her features, and how no matter what, she would never be able to wear a bikini because of stretch marks dating back to sixth grade, or something like that. So he just refused to comment at all. "The car ride home was a bitch, though," he groaned, though a hint of a smile flashed across his features. "I decided that since I had a couple hours, it was time to call my mom."

Donna gasped, but she could tell that the story was going to be humorous.

"Don't worry; I told her she was forbidden to drag you into it." Kenny pointed his finger, reenacting how stern he had been.

Donna smiled.

"Anyway, it wasn't too bad after she got over the initial shock and quit asking if I was sure."

"That's so crazy. She's disappointed that you're not gay. It fits your mother, though. How'd your dad take it?"

"Well, I didn't actually talk to him because mom wouldn't give up the phone, but I think he's celebrating inwardly." Kenny laughed as he pictured the sight. "It's too bad, though. Here I had some of the most accepting parents ever, and they never really had anything to accept. I feel kinda guilty."

"Not to fall Freudian, or anything, but don't you think your mother's 'acceptance' was more like pushiness? I mean, if she hadn't been so eager for you to be gay, do you think you would have lived that way so long?"

"I know. Actually, I am positive that her encouragement kept me thinking it's what I was all that time. Looking back, there were so many clues in the way she treated me and in the way I felt toward Marcos."

Donna felt awkward at the mention of his name. She did not know if she should say something comforting to Kenny, or out of respect toward Marcos. She was afraid that continuing about his mother might upset him even more. She decided to let the moment fade and move on to a completely new subject.

"Oh, guess what?" Donna said with sudden gusto a moment later.

"What?" Kenny said, imitating her enthusiasm.

"Cam and I totally got rollerblades yesterday," she yipped.

"No way," said Kenny, not knowing if he was allowed to laugh, or if she was expecting him to ignore the fact that she was the least coordinated person he had ever met.

"I know, and I admit that I totally suck." She smiled big, but did not lose her zeal. "Cam is really good though, and he is teaching me. At least I am better than when I first tried them on in the store," she added to rebut Kenny's disbelieving face.

"Well, it is good that you want to exercise and be fit," Kenny finally decided it was safe to say.

"What about you?" asked Donna, looking at him.

Kenny shrugged.

"I mean, now that you and Tianna are over, whatcha gonna do with yourself?"

Kenny blew out a long sigh. "I don't know. Truthfully, I think I could do without a new girlfriend for a while. Maybe I'll just start going to strip clubs. Isn't that what straight guys do?"

Donna gave him a 'that's not funny' kind of look.

"Whatever. Like you thought for a second that I would."

Donna made a face, rolling her eyes up and to the side, twisting her lips upward and shrugging her shoulders in a 'who knows' fashion.

By the end of their date, Donna knew that Kenny was going to be all right.

Cameron and Donna's first date anniversary was finally upon them. It seemed odd to have half their wedding planned already. Donna had to fight with him to put his seatbelt on, as usual, though she had noticed he had been doing it of his own volition more often than not. He told her he just 'wasn't raised that way,' but she always vowed that, as their kids would be raised that way, he had better start getting used to it.

"One of these days, you're gonna run headlong into a pole, go flying through the windshield, and I'll never see you again," she predicted grimly.

"I'll put the f'in' belt on," he said with an exasperated laugh.

"Well, it could happen," Donna upheld.

"God, you're sexy," he said all of a sudden, stroking her leg with his fingertip, staring into her eyes with a gleam in his own.

Donna blushed. Though the comment made her feel obvious, she did not chastise him for changing the subject. When he turned back to the driveway, however, she fixed her skirt so that it fell longer past her thighs. She also tugged the waist up a little higher to prevent any roll spillage, wondering why she had not chosen something a little looser, knowing she would be holding back nothing at this meal. *If only it was possible not to have to sit in certain outfits*, she thought.

"Well, thank God there's no more Kenny and Tianna to deal with," Cameron sighed, speaking freely.

"Yeah. That was such a mess."

"So, are you going to have a funeral for the eggplant?" he smirked.

"Actually, I was thinking about approaching Tony with a back-door exchange proposition."

They both laughed.

"Well, they won't have eggplant parmesan where we are going tonight, but it is one of your favorite places—though I don't think we've ever actually been there together."

Donna rubbed her hands in anticipation. "I can't wait to find out."

After fifteen minutes of food fantasies floating through her head, Donna was excited to find that Cameron was indeed pulling into the parking lot of one of her favorite restaurants.

"This better not be a fake-out," she warned.

"It's the real deal," he promised smugly.

"You're trying to get me drunk, aren't you? You know the best ever sake-tini is made just inside those doors, don't you?"

Cameron gave an impish grin and leaned in to kiss her, not letting her go for a long, ardent moment.

It was nearly impossible for Donna to believe that someone out there could admire her physical beauty without being facetious, yet Cameron's words and actions evidenced his genuine lust for her every day. It was one thing she had never expected. Though she had always longed for her one true love, she had never expected the lust that would come with it.

"**K**enny, do you think we'll ever get married?" Donna asked him one day as a young teenager.

"I don't know." He sounded doubtful.

"I can't imagine anyone could ever want to marry me."

"I probably don't have a great chance at it, either," he commiserated.

"I think if we're thirty and unmarried, we should attempt spontaneous combustion," Donna proposed seriously.

"Doesn't attempting it mean it's not spontaneous?"

Donna shrugged. "Well, we know some of the possible factors that cause it—if we put ourselves under the best circumstances for it, maybe it would happen."

"There's what—cold weather, high levels of static electricity, obesity—"

Donna, nodding along with his list, patted her belly, and said, "One down!"

Kenny rolled his eyes, but did not comment.

"So, we have to get really fat, fly to Siberia in the coldest part of winter, and learn how to generate high levels of static electricity," Donna stated as though it would be simple to accomplish.

"What if it didn't work and we were just fat and cold?" Kenny wondered.

Donna seemed indifferent. "Then we could come back to America and know that we'd given it a shot."

"Or we could stay and learn Chinese," he suggested thoughtfully. "The Russian side is *too* cold."

"Either way." Donna shrugged.

4

Much to Kenny's disbelief, Donna was still going strong on her rollerblades two months later. Though she had had random lapses of routine, she had been fairly consistent in going anywhere from two to five times a week. She did not know if it was helping to get her body wedding dress-ready, but she liked it, and it made her feel like she was accomplishing *something*. Kenny liked watching her skate along like an unsteady five-year-old, sure to fall at any moment, yet managing somehow to stay on her feet. He had started riding his bike alongside her sometimes, though he generally just rode around a bit, then came back to her, as there was no way she could keep up.

After one such session, Kenny and Donna were having refreshments, silly, slightly out of breath, and a bit sweaty.

"Maybe I should just get a skateboard. Then we'd be more even," Kenny thought out loud.

"Remember what assholes all those skater guys in high school were?" Donna said, as though she still held a grudge.

Kenny made a sound of indignant agreement. "If only I had known then I wasn't gay. I would have taken a lot less shit from those guys."

Donna nodded. "I never got why so many girls fawned over them. Some were good looking—don't get me wrong, but who could stand their arrogance, and how 'punk rock' they thought they were?"

"I know. Some of them thought they would actually have pro-skater careers. It must suck to be those guys now. Somehow, being a good skater doesn't get you near as far as a couple of years of college—if any of those jackasses even graduated."

"Well, there were also the ones that just liked to skate, but weren't assholes, or if they were, it was more for comical purposes than anything else," Donna countered.

Kenny gave a look, as though to admit that they were not all jerks. "I wasn't saying that they all sucked, but the ones that did, really did."

"I just never understood, I guess. I mean, not just the skaters, but also in the rest of high school society. I've never understood idolizing the most ridiculous people in the school, whether they were macho jocks, rebels, musicians, or whatever. I just never felt the urge to go 'woo-hoo!' And it seems that you have to be that type to get it."

Kenny laughed a little, but he knew what she was saying. "I suppose apathy does that to you. Wouldn't it have been nice to have been able to get excited about stupid things like that? The people who did feel that way seemed to have so much to live for. Sometimes I wished pep assemblies were important, that SAT's were worth stressing over, that it mattered if our team won the game. It would have made life so much livelier."

"Yeah. We're just the jaded, outcast observers that scoffed at everything, which may have entailed some mild entertainment, but mostly just sucked. Wouldn't it have been great to feel, whether we were totally lame or not? I don't get what happened between middle school and high school that caused us to lose that. Remember how giddy we used to be?" Kenny nodded along with her. "Remember playing MistaSista?" Donna laughed so hard, she could barely pronounce the title.

Kenny laughed, too. "Oh, the shame!" he acted out melodramatically.

MistaSista was the name of Kenny and Donna's pretend talk show, in which Kenny wore a red feather boa and played hostess to panels of various social misfits. Donna alternated between panel and audience members, and announced the show.

"I still can't believe you ever got me on camera. I cried the first time I saw how blotchy and blubbery I looked on film. I totally hated it."

"I still want to feel like that sometimes, too," Kenny sighed. "I wish there was something I cared about. Even if it was just daily life. I wish I could just make myself not only do, but want to do things like make my bed in the morning. Why is it so hard to open every piece of mail when I get it, and not just pick out the bills and leave the rest on the counter?"

"I know. I want to be a real person, too. I'm afraid of it, but sometimes when I come home and the house is really messy, I get so depressed. I didn't grow up like that—you know how my dad was. If one glass was left out, he'd have a fit, and now my whole coffee table will be full of glasses," she waved her hand over the table to show her example, "and I hate it, but I still do nothing until Saturday, when I make myself do it because it's just so out of hand again. Then I ask Cam to help, and it's like I'm playing Mom, because he's even worse than I am," Donna sighed, frustrated. "He always reacts as though I am attacking him, when I just want us both to be better people. I want us to become real, so we can have kids and raise them well, and be happier, better people."

"Sometimes I'm afraid that I never will, either. I don't know if people who never went 'woo-hoo' can become real. I think we might be doomed."

"Well, it's not like I care about community involvement, and God knows I would never run for HOA officer, local government, or anything crazy like that; I just want to take care of myself—of us—of our family, eventually. I want to have a retirement fund and a college fund for our kids. I want to feel secure like I did under my parents' roof." Donna was being so honest, she felt like she might cry if she continued. "I know we're not even married yet, but since we're going to be, these things are important. If we don't work to change now, we never will. I'll always feel bogged down by my own apathy, and I hate that."

Kenny looked at her for a long moment. It had been some time since they had delved so deeply into each other's woes. First, he was no longer gay, now Donna was desperate to become real. "Maybe these are the first signs," he said hopefully. "I guess if you aren't born real, then you have to become it." He shrugged. "Have you ever been so used to hanging out with people like us that sometimes when you are talking to someone you don't really know it suddenly occurs to you that they are a real person, and you have no business wasting their time?" He kinda laughed.

"It happens a lot in interviews." Donna concurred with a smile. "All of the sudden, mid-sentence, you have to try to play it as though you are real too, or you completely lose their interest."

The atmosphere suddenly seemed much lighter. Donna got up from her loveseat with much effort. "Want anything while I am up?"

Kenny shook his head. Donna threw the remote to him, indicating that he should choose a show to watch. "Cam must be working late," she said, observing the time on the microwave clock as she entered the kitchen. She thought it odd that he had not called to tell her, as he was normally so considerate.

"Ooh!" Kenny cried, putting down the remote after going through half the stations and finding nothing on. "Let's watch your *Golden Girls,* season III!"

Donna suddenly became enthusiastic herself.

After a few minutes to settle back in and belt out the song, they were watching their classic, favorite show. Anyone viewing the scene from the outside might have doubted Kenny's recent pronouncement.

"This show is better than comfort food." Donna pronounced, making herself comfortable on her stomach, chin supported in her palms.

"They eat all the cheesecakes and sundaes for you." Kenny grinned.

It was not until the girls found out that "Baby" was a pig in the third episode that Donna noticed the time again; Cam still had not called. "I'm gonna check my phone. Maybe I just left it on silent again," she said, getting up from the floor, massaging her arm, which had fallen asleep and was beginning to cramp.

Donna found her purse on the kitchen table, half-hidden in the midst of her despised disarray of debris. There were no message indicators on, and the phone was not set to silent.

"I don't normally get freaked out, but this is not like him," she said, punching a number into the phone.

Kenny muted the show. He could not sit there and enjoy it without knowing what was going on, either.

Donna waited, pacing and tapping her fingers against the table. After a minute or so, she left a message that was quick and forceful, but not too urgent. Without looking back to Kenny, she punched in another number and turned her back to him, focusing on nothing but what she could hear through the phone, hoping for a voice. All she got was another machine. She sighed heavily and put her phone in her pocket.

"Let's keep watching. I'm sure he just stopped by his parents' house or something and didn't think to call me."

Kenny did not speak, but gave her an 'are you sure?' look. She nodded as she returned to the floor beside him, though this time her posture was much more rigid.

Sometime during the sixth episode, Donna's phone finally rang. Looking at the display before answering, she saw Cameron's cell phone number and breathed a sigh of relief.

"Hello."

"Donna?" came someone other than Cameron's voice in a very serious tone.

"Yes," she replied, suddenly uncertain.

Kenny, noticing her tone, muted the show again.

"Donna, this is Greg, Cameron's old fraternity buddy. We took him out for dinner after work tonight, and—" he sniffled. "There's been an accident. I was DD, so there was no DUI involved, but—"

Donna gasped. Kenny dashed to her side, searching for any indication of what she was being told.

"Cam—" Greg made a high-pitched, whining squeal, like he was doing all he could not to break down.

"Yes, yes—what is it?" Donna fretted.

There were odd, muffled sounds of the phone being passed around, and when a speaker finally returned, it was Cameron's other friend, Jay. "I'm sorry, honey," he began, only slightly more stable than Greg. "Cameron's passed on. We were hit on the freeway, and he wasn't wearing his seatbelt. He went through the windshield and died almost instantly."

Donna was crying so hard that she was not making a sound, though tears streamed down her face. She was straining so hard that it pained her, but still could not relent.

Jay waited patiently, trying to be strong on the other end of the line. Donna set the phone on the floor, and Kenny came around to hold her. "I want to die," she wept. "I want to be dead."

Kenny found the phone on floor. He brought it to his ear and mouth, still holding Donna.

"Hi. This is Donna's friend, Kenny. Is there anything further?"

"Not really, no. I'm sure we'll hear more about the burial." Kenny's heart plummeted. "But we just needed to tell Donna. We only had his parents' info at first, so they'll get the next wave of information, and pass it on. All of us were unharmed; I just thought to check Cam's cell for Donna's number."

"Okay."

"Tell her we're sorry, and that she can call Cam's parents for anything at all."

"Okay," Kenny said again. "Thanks for calling. I'm sure once she has had some time she will want to know more."

As he clamped the phone shut, he felt that it was like Marcos all over again. He hated himself for comparing his situation to Donna's, but he could not help it.

He had let her go while on the phone, and now watched her on her knees, head bowed, letting out an occasional squeak between silent sobs. "What can I do for you, sweetie?" he asked, lifting her chin with his finger.

Donna shook her chin from his grip and bowed her head again, not responding. "Okay, honey," he said softly. "I'm gonna be right behind you on the couch. I'll stay as long as you like."

Donna nodded to the carpet. She put one hand out feebly toward him. He took it and held it for a long moment. It fell limply when he let go. He crawled onto the couch behind her awkwardly, giving her hair a little stroke once he was situated. Donna stayed where she was for a short time, then eventually crept on her knees in his direction, until she was level with his chest, and fell upon him. Kenny held her in his arms and kissed her pate, comforting her until he fell asleep.

Donna fell asleep, too, but she awoke before Kenny and maneuvered awkwardly out of his arms. Her face hurt from all the crying she had done. It was still dark out, but she had no idea what time it was. Leaving Kenny asleep on the couch, she grabbed her purse and exited the apartment.

A short time later, Donna arrived at an all night deli. She entered slowly, not aware of what was going on around her. She shivered as she waited at the hostess station, then realizing she was holding a jacket, she put it on clumsily. It was off-kilter, covering one side and falling off the other shoulder. Donna made a vague attempt to fix it, but gave up almost at once.

The hostess took in her glassy-eyed appearance, feeling cautious, but not too wary to seat her. Donna thanked her and took the menu without looking at her. She set the menu on the table, but did not open it. She rested her chin on her palm, elbow on the table, and stared at nothing.

She was starting to draw the attention of another customer, who had looked up from the laptop before him and taken in her deportment with keen interest. He kept quiet, observing, finding himself unable to go back to work. He continued to watch her for several moments, during which a waitress tried to take her drink order, but Donna refused to answer.

Finally, the manager of the restaurant was brought to her table; he began talking to her in his most delicate tone. "Miss? Miss?"

Donna did not answer, did not even turn to look at him. If anything, she slouched even further and gave a meager hiccup.

The young man with the laptop was more intrigued than ever. He had a studious look about him, black framed glasses, neat, wavy blonde hair, and an inquisitive gleam in his eye.

"Honey, I'm sorry, but you've got to say something, or I'm afraid you can't stay here," the manager tried again.

Donna made a jerky movement to face him at last.

The manager waited for her to speak.

"I killed my husband," she finally revealed, eyes still unfocused.

The manager and the staff that had begun to gather jumped back.

"I killed him." She shrugged, as though she had run an errand on the way over to the deli.

Stepping back further, the manager whispered to the waitress from the corner of his mouth, "Go dial 9-1-1."

Terrified, the waitress went on command, without replying.

Donna's observer, however, leapt to his feet at the proclamation and approached. The manager tried to keep him away, but he just held up a hand, and came nearer.

"Hi," he said simply.

"Hi," said Donna, beginning to sob.

"Are you okay?"

"My husband is dead, and I killed him," she reiterated, looking guilty.

"How'd it happen?" the stranger asked, as though she had not just confessed to murder.

"A car wreck," Donna said in a baby voice. "He never wears his seatbelt. I told him it was going to happen, and it did. He's dead—went right through the windshield, just like I said."

"Do I know you?" he asked, climbing into the booth opposite her.

Donna looked at him, focusing for the first time since she had entered the deli. "You're Josh Addington, one of those asshole skaters we were talking about earlier," she said abruptly.

The young man looked down. "You must have known me in high school," he admitted.

"You made fun of Kenny every day, and guess what—he's not even gay."

"I know. I was a total loser back then—" he began, but then realized who she was. "Donna DiSimone?" he said with disbelief.

"Yeah," she said. "I'm not fat, and Kenny's not gay."

The manager was utterly befuddled. He signaled the waitress that had gone to call 9-1-1 to hold off.

"You're beautiful," Josh said, breathless.

Donna rolled her eyes. "I only look different."

"I look pretty much the same," said Josh, "but I am a different person."

Donna had forgotten all about Cameron for the moment. She was full of rage toward Josh, whom she really did not even know, but was a symbol of all she hated.

Just then, the bell on the door jingled, and everyone jumped again. Kenny entered the place without waiting to speak to a hostess, frantically searching the tables, finding Donna easily.

Kenny sighed a huge breath of relief, jogging to meet her. "What are you doing here?" he said like a father who had found his lost child.

Donna turned to him, and snapped out of her distant mood. She looked around, wondering the same thing. "I don't know."

It was as though she had come out of a trance. She looked at Josh as if she had no idea that she had been sitting with him, much less talking with him. She recognized him instantly, though, and jumped in surprise.

"What's he doing here?" she asked Kenny, as though he ought to know.

Then Kenny also recognized him and started a bit too. "Come on, Donna, let's go home." He watched Josh suspiciously the whole time it took for Donna to chivy out of the booth, stand up, and take his hand, which he pulled her away with a bit roughly.

"No. Wait!" Josh cried out.

Kenny looked confused. "What do you want with her?"

"I don't know," Josh admitted quietly.

"Okay, then, let's go," said Kenny more forcefully, tugging Donna by the hand again. He turned to the manager apologetically. "I'm sorry for whatever happened. I'll take care of her, and we'll come back for her car tomorrow. I know it's parked kinda funny—but I'll come as early as possible."

The manager, glad to have the episode over with, nodded profusely, ushering them out.

Josh wanted to beg them not to leave, but there was no reason for them to stay. It was obvious that she needed familiar comfort, not some stranger prying into her troubles. No matter how stunned he had been by her, he had to put it aside.

Another wave of clarity came over Donna as she said, "Wait!" For one brief moment, Josh thought she was going to beg him not to stay behind, but instead she said, "Can we get a to-go order?"

Kenny rolled his eyes and dragged her out, muttering, "We'll hit a drive-thru."

When they got outside, Donna understood what Kenny meant about her car. Apparently, Donna had decided that the designated parking spots were optional. She had parked sideways, with her front tires in the planter bordering the spots.

"I can't believe no one pulled me over for a DUI, if that's how I was driving," she commented, realizing how crazy she had been.

"How do you think I knew you were here? I came here to check the liquor store on the corner, but then I saw that," Kenny explained.

"The liquor store? You make me sound like a wino." Donna was offended.

"Well, in truth, it was the cigarettes, not the liquor, I was worried about. I heard the car, I knew you'd just left, and I was afraid you would relapse," he admitted.

"I probably would have, but my mind never made it that far."

"Well, come on now. Let's just go back home." He put an arm around her, escorting her toward his car.

"Kenny," she began with difficulty, "if I promise to be sane, could we please go somewhere to eat?"

He took a good look at her, and saw a change. She no longer seemed lost, but solemn, and the desire to go anywhere but home was evident in her features.

"Okay," he agreed, as though his permission had been required. "I don't think we can go back in the deli without scaring the crap out of everyone in there, so let's just go to Denny's. They don't know us there yet."

Donna smiled as she cozied up to him. She loved Kenny, and knew he would always take care of her. As they drove away, though, Donna looked back at the deli. Staring out of one of the enormous front windows was Josh, looking like a puppy whose owner was leaving on a long vacation. She gave a little smile as Kenny picked up speed, not knowing if Josh was able to see it. She would think about his presence later, when she had the strength. Right then, all she wanted was to fill her belly then hibernate for a good eighteen hours.

Donna sat at the diner with a little more life in her than there had been on the drive over, but she skimmed the dinner menu with little interest.

"This is a time for biscuits and gravy," she stated wearily.

Kenny smiled to himself, not wanting to flood her with conversation.

"Maybe every day should be," Donna said thoughtfully. "Maybe I should just regain all the weight, and then some. Boys could go back to ignoring me, and I could revel in my own misery again. That life was safer."

Again, Kenny kept to himself. It was not until a minute later that Donna gave an involuntary snort of laughter, and a huge smile broke from between her lips, engaging her entire face in laughter.

"I could be in the *Enquirer* for literally eating myself out of house and home—then, wait—I could come up with a diet, use it to return to an even slimmer version of my former self. They could call the article, 'A Literal Glutton for Punishment.'"

Kenny could not contain himself. Laughing heartily, he said, "The sad thing is—it's probably true."

"Eat something made of lard and sugar—we can go in on this together," Donna beamed.

"But what about Siberia?" he asked, as though this new plan would negate their old one.

Donna looked thoughtful. Twisting her lips to the side, her forefinger pressed to them, she took an antsy moment of contemplation.

"Okay. Siberia is too great to pass up. The diet will have to take the back burner. We'll start saving everything we have now, apply it toward buffet after buffet—we may need to move to Vegas for this to pan out, somehow get to Siberia—we should totally start a website for sponsorship—then what? Walk around in the snow after rubbing our feet on the carpet, and hope we blow up?"

Kenny was having convulsions by this point, he was laughing so hard. "I guess. How long do we wait, though? What if only one of us combusts?"

"Then both possibilities would be fulfilled." Donna's face shone as she considered it for the first time. "Whoever stays intact would go on to build the diet empire."

The conversation was exactly what was needed to ease their spirits after such a trying evening. They ate merrily, putting their grief in the backs of their minds for the night.

The next morning, Kenny got up early, intending to retrieve Donna's car from the planter in front of the deli. She was already awake, apparently having resumed *The Golden Girls* only a few minutes prior, as she was still on the episode they had last been on the night before.

"Some people remember where they were the day Kennedy got shot. I'll always remember the terrible coat Dorothy Zbornak was wearing as she addressed the Russian public in Rose's dream the night Cam flew out the windshield," she said somberly upon hearing Kenny enter the living room, not looking at him.

Kenny sighed. He had almost forgotten the tragedy of the night before. "I know, sweetie." He sat next to her, leaning gingerly on her shoulder for comfort. "Are you going to call Cameron's mom today?"

Donna looked grim. "I don't know—I mean, what do I say? I barely know her, but I don't want to wait around wondering if she'll call me…" Donna trailed off in consternation.

"Sorry. I shouldn't have brought it up." Kenny bowed his head.

"No. No, it's not that. I know you want to make sure I am keeping as level-headed as possible." She paused. "I just can't believe I'm not getting married. I have no idea what the future *is* any more." Donna threw her hands into the couch on either side of her, nearly hitting Kenny, at this pronouncement. "I just keep seeing a mental image of the phrase 'all sewn up' being deconstructed, a giant zipper being pulled open, and all this matter oozing out. I can't even say what it's falling out of— perhaps a burlap sack—kinda like Mr. Oogie Boogie unraveling."

Kenny smiled, enjoying the image and seeing how it fit her predicament.

"I guess I always look toward the future. I always seem to be waiting for some event to take place, then I go on to the next one. I never enjoy what I have. Perhaps that's my problem. Maybe I didn't enjoy Cam enough while he was here. I was so set on our wedding, our house, our kids, our twenty-fifth anniversary party—"

When it seemed appropriate to change the subject, Kenny brought her to today. "Do you think you can drive this morning, or would you rather I walked over to the deli and brought your car back?"

Donna shrugged. "I'll drive."

Kenny breathed a sigh of relief, as it would have taken him about twenty minutes to walk that far; he gave her a few minutes to get ready. Waiting outside for her, he took in the cool morning air. The valley was in its short transition between winter and summer, which were the only real seasons it seemed to have. The weather would only be beautiful for about two weeks before the heat came. He wished his heart were more in the mood to enjoy it. Donna soon exited the apartment, locked up, and gave a half smile to Kenny as she followed him to his car.

When they arrived at the deli a couple minutes later, Donna gasped at the sight of her car. "Thank God it's only five a.m. This would be hell to own up to in couple of hours when the lot is full."

"Let me get it onto the road for you," said Kenny as he killed the ignition and jumped out of his seat a few spots away.

He put a hand out for her keys.

Donna obliged wordlessly.

The car jerked a little, and there was a loud bump as the wheels hit the asphalt, but it was an easy dismount. Kenny left the car running, waiting by the door until she got in. "You gonna be okay from here?"

Donna nodded, feeling sheepish.

"Okay, I'll follow you back. It will only be a minute."

As he walked back to his car, Donna noticed a note under her windshield wiper and reached awkwardly around to the front to remove it. It was a white, letter-sized page folded into thirds—hardly the type of advertisement she would expect. She looked back to Kenny, making sure he was not watching before opening it. She had no reason to believe it was something secret, but there was a portentous feeling about it, all the same.

Unfolding the page, she saw a letter written on it, but something else distracted her. It was a poem—not any poem—

one she had written ten years ago in creative writing class with Kenny. She tucked it away as Kenny pulled up next to her.

"You *are* up to this, right?"

"Yeah. Yeah, I'm fine. I was just thinking."

"Well, go on then. I'll follow you, just in case."

Donna nodded and went to start the car before remembering it was already running. Once she was finally off, she tried to pay attention to the road, but could not stop from going back to the letter. She could not wait to get a moment alone so she could read it. It had to have been left by Josh the night before, but why would he have her old poem?

Night

Night is a Gothic, and stars
  are his hair.
He laughs a full moon,
And crescents a smirk.
 His eyes are the sinister,
    grey
  clouds, haunting
      The moor.

That face of Night, the
  Gothic face!
All painted up and gleaming
        so.

  His face the mask,
  His anger thunders,
   And fears, they rain,
  As he does not like what
      is below.

    "Death and Poetry"

5

Kenny and Donna were back at her place in a matter of minutes, wishing that they had been clever enough to get breakfast while they were out. They had just settled on baking a frozen pizza when they heard the sound of someone outside trying to use a key.

Confused, Donna inched hesitantly toward the door, straining to hear. Kenny watched from a few yards away as the door opened and Cameron sleepily entered the house with a guilty look on his face.

Kenny could not believe his eyes. He had to hold Donna upright as she wobbled haphazardly upon recognizing her reportedly dead fiancé.

"I know you're probably pissed as hell that I didn't call, but honestly, I didn't plan to be more than hour with the guys last night, then things got out of hand, and I wound up plowed on the floor before it was even late."

Donna was sheet-white, staring at him incredulously.

"Please don't be mad at me, Donna. The guys bombarded me at the office, and they wouldn't let me phone you before I left. Then Greg stole my phone. The next thing I knew, I was barely alive in the back of someone's car, trying to wait until I got out to puke. Poor excuse for a surprise bachelor party, I know, but that's what happened." He finally sighed, dropping his hands to his side.

Donna choked on her own breath.

Kenny did not know if he should hold her or let her be. "Wow!" he said in awed amazement. "You have no idea, do you?"

Cameron was stunned by the severity of his tone. He turned around to see who was behind him, not conceiving how Kenny's comment could have been directed at him. When he did, however, Kenny got a better understanding of what was going on. Cameron turned back to them, shrugging.

"Turn the other way for a moment," Kenny ordered him.

Cameron looked at him oddly.

"I'm not checking out your ass," Kenny snipped. "There's something written on the back of your shirt."

Cameron looked confused, but did it anyway, craning his neck, trying to read it for himself at the same time.

HE'S ALIVE! was printed in large, lighting bolt shaped letters, then in smaller ones underneath, it said, APRIL FOOL'S!

Donna's face began to melt into sobs. It was so cruel—so incomprehensible. She ran to the couch, and Cameron ran after her.

"How could I not have realized the date?" Donna clapped a hand to her forehead. "Not that there's *any* excuse for it, but maybe I would have thought twice about it if I had realized. Stupid me—leaving April Fool's pranks in grade school."

"Thank God you never called his mother," Kenny said with a chastising look at Cameron.

"Why don't you tell me what happened. Then I'll figure out whose ass to kick."

Donna huffed. "You apparently have no idea went on, so I'm doing my best to quell my desire to strangle you myself."

Kenny excused himself almost immediately after that and headed out.

It was almost too much for Donna to put into words how she felt and what had happened.

"Greg called, and he said you'd been in an accident. Then Jay got on because Greg was supposedly too overcome with grief to continue. Apparently, he knows you well because he said you weren't buckled, which is why you went through the windshield; I felt so guilty for all the times I told you that you would one day."

"That sick fuck," Cameron grunted. "Those assholes didn't even have the balls to tell me this morning. They must have gotten your number out of my phone and called while I was passed out." He had his head in his hands, unable to see the humor in the act. "God, what if you had called my parents?"

"Why would I doubt the news? It's a fact of communicative nature that people believe what they are told unless there is some kind of sign that makes them suspicious. The call was just so quick." Shaking her head, she groaned vigorously. "I can just picture them *dying* laughing upon hanging up."

Even Cameron could not believe how low his friends had gone this time. "Not a single one of those jackasses will be at the wedding."

"Wedding?" asked Donna. The word caught her off guard. That was right. There was still going to be a wedding. Her future had not been spoiled, had not changed, Mr. Oogie Boogie was zipping back up.

"Yeah. Forget that. You just don't do that to someone," Cameron fumed.

"I could see if they had told the truth at the end of the call, or called back to explain the joke, but all night, I thought you were gone." Donna looked around, trying to find the words. "If Kenny hadn't been there, I might have killed myself. It was my first thought."

"Donna," Cameron breathed, on the verge of crying.

"Plus, what total shit for Kenny to endure so soon after Marcos. He must have felt like we had something to share—our closest friends dying, and us left behind to blow up in Siberia."

For the first time, 'death and poetry' crossed her mind, as if it was a morbid theme describing her life of late.

If Cameron found the last of her postulation odd, he did not show it. "Donna, please don't leave me. I promise I had no idea what they did." He removed his shirt and threw it to the ground in one swift movement, as though he could not stand to be covered in the joke a moment longer. "I couldn't take it if you did." He was curled around her arm now, clinging on like a dependent lifeform.

"You are my limpet." She smiled down at him, stroking his arm.

He curled closer to her, close enough to make her squirm, afraid he would notice her tummy fat, especially since the midnight feast at Denny's had extended it beyond its normal consistency.

He pawed at her lovingly, indicating she should shift to cuddle with him. "You really would have killed yourself?"

"I don't know," Donna sniffed. "I couldn't see what was worth living for if my one true love was gone."

They lay together for a long time after, not speaking, and not thinking, just glad to have each other.

Into that night and the next day, something about the exchange did not sit right with Donna. Cameron had seemed genuinely unaware of the prank and pissed off that it had been played, and that much was okay. The part that bothered Donna was the fact that Cameron had not called her and told her that he was going out. Sure, he said they would not let him use his phone, but Donna had to wonder. No matter what jerks these old friends apparently were, at some point they would have let him call home. Donna doubted they threatened to kill him if he tried. Beyond that, he should have been able to find another phone somewhere. It only would have taken a minute to leave her a message, or say, "Sorry, I can't talk. I hate to do this, but I'm gonna be out late tonight because some friends dropped by unexpectedly." Then, Donna might have had a little heads-up about the whole thing.

Plus, Cameron had called it a bachelor party. Did that mean there were strippers and who knew what else, too? It seemed that the kind of guys that would play such tricks would also hire strippers or drag him out to a nudie bar. Her decision now rested on to what degree she believed Cameron should be held responsible for his behavior. Given that he was, for the most part, unaware of what was going on, should his tale be considered the truth? One factor she could not deny was that Kenny never would have gone out without calling if the two of them had had plans. *Shouldn't my husband be more considerate, or at least as considerate, as my best friend?* she could not avoid thinking. *What if we had kids and something like this happened? Could I really marry someone who had anything in common with those guys? What if Cameron thought it was funny at the time and was only pretending to have been in the dark about it because I reacted so badly? What if the T-shirt had been Cameron's idea?*

Donna did not know what to do. Was this worth giving up her marriage? Would she be better off without him, knowing how flippantly he handled an issue she saw as important? Even if the worst was true—if Cameron had done this horrible thing intentionally—was it fair to break off their engagement, if he had learned from it and was truly sorry? What if she did forgive him, though? Would she be setting herself up for a greater disappointment down the line? It seemed there was no good decision to be made. Maybe their engagement had been too rushed, after all.

More to distract herself than anything else, Donna went back to the note Josh left her the night before. She left Cameron playing a computer game in their office and took the letter to her bedroom. Curled up comfortably and leaning back with her sitting-up pillow against her headboard for support, she unfolded the paper and took in its contents with analytical interest.

Across the top of the paper was printed, "I never forgot…" Underneath that was her poem, Xeroxed from the original typed version she had handed in, in tenth grade, for the end-of-year poetry collection. Donna was touched that he must have gone home, extracted the book from beneath a decade of memorabilia, copied the poem—most likely at the Kinko's next to the deli, she thought—wrote the note, and tucked it under her wiper blade, all between eleven p.m. and five a.m. the night before.

The note read,

Donna, please meet me here again tonight. Don't judge me by who I used to be. I'd really like to talk to you. I have always been

inspired by this poem and can hardly believe I ran into you after all these years. I'll be at the deli at eight p.m., hoping to see you there.
-jla

Donna almost cried. The note was short, but seemed sincere. She felt an odd dip, then numbness in her heart, and wondered if the feeling might be love. If it was love, was she cheating on Cam by going to meet Josh?

Getting out of the house that night was easy for Donna. Cameron had been walking around the house on eggshells all day, and the tension made being apart from each other for a while a potential source of relief.

Josh was waiting for Donna in front of the bakery counter in the deli's foyer. She was almost surprised to see him, feeling in the back of her mind that this was another fraternity stunt—meet the ugly girl for a date, get her all excited, and humiliate her in front of everyone. She did not think she would be able to handle it twice in under twenty-four hours. All she could do, though, was walk up to him, wishing that her butterflies would die down.

"You came," he said in a happy tone.

"Yeah," Donna breathed, knowing how nervous she sounded.

They walked over to the hostess stand. Donna was glad to see that it was a different girl than the one the night before. No words were exchanged, only odd, hesitant glances and smiles as they were seated.

Right off the bat, the waitress asked Josh if he would like his usual pot of regular with cream and sugar. He accepted with a look toward Donna, who indicated she would have coffee too.

"You must come here a lot," Donna started, observing how familiar the staff was with him.

"Actually, I do. I come in late at night to work and drink coffee." He laughed at himself. "Plus, I used to work here—for about two years."

"Really?" Donna asked, genuinely questioning the validity of the statement.

Josh nodded, finding her disbelief humorous.

"It's just that I have come here a lot myself, apparently not as much as you have, but I think I would have recognized you at some point."

He shrugged. "I could probably have my employee file pulled if you really wanted proof."

Donna reached across the table to smack him playfully. When they touched, her heart dipped again, and she suddenly felt guilty for even being there. Still, she could not persuade herself to leave. "It must have been during my years at U of A. We must have just missed each other."

Josh smiled, accepting her assumption.

Donna cleared her throat as a preface to her change of subject a moment later. "Before we get into our conversation, I want to clear up what happened last night." She gulped.

Josh's face fell a little. He knew his eagerness to see her again had not been very sensitive to her recent loss.

"Well, as it turns out," she said, sounding embarrassed, "my 'husband' is not actually dead." Donna pronounced the "H" word with a bit more feeling than she had known was coming. "I just had the cruelest joke in the world played on me. I was told that my fiancé had died in a car accident, but he was actually passed out at buddy's house. I didn't know until he made his way home a little after five a.m. this morning."

Josh's jaw dropped. "What?"

"Yeah," Donna said, not believing it herself, though she had just been through it.

"Not April Fool's?" he asked incredulously.

"Yep," Donna nodded.

"Wow! I'm sorry, but I just can't imagine—"

Donna shook her head. She would not have been able to imagine such a thing herself if it had not just happened to her. She plunged into the story of how it had started and ended.

"Not wanting to overstep my boundaries, but I don't buy that crap about him 'not being able to call.' Unless he's a total wuss, he probably thought he wouldn't be out too late, and he'd get away with not calling, but when he woke up so much later, he felt guilty and ran home." Josh commented. "Apart from the fact that I like to think of myself as a considerate person, I can't imagine not telling my fiancée I wouldn't be home. Is this typical behavior for him?"

"No—and that's the thing. I'm sure that his buddies did influence him, but at the same time, is that an acceptable excuse? I just don't know anymore. If I think we should break up, then I feel petty, as if I just wanted out and used this as an excuse. If I think we should get past this, he learned his lesson, was immature, and won't behave like that again, I wonder if this isn't the big warning sign, and we'll be divorced in a year, just like so many other young couples."

'Troubled' was all Josh could think as he watched her, taking in her movements, noticing the tiniest details as her facial expressions changed.

"I take it this is the first time you have had doubts about him," Josh remarked sagely.

Donna looked up. "How did you know?"

"I can tell." He shrugged. "Certain things you said, the degree to which you want to give him the benefit of the doubt..."

Donna was amazed by his ability to read her.

He looked at her intently for a moment, reached out to take her hands, and said, "You're very *real*, Donna. It's what first drew me to you. You've become my muse. Until I left to come here tonight, I have not stopped writing since I saw you twenty hours ago."

Donna liked his use of the word real. He meant it very differently than she generally did when using it with Kenny—as an actor might, she thought—but the double-entendre still seemed to apply. He meant that not only was she up-front and truthful about her thoughts and emotions, but also that she was a *real* person, entitled to acknowledgement. Never forgetting she was still betrothed, however, she could not allow herself to become swept away.

"Writing?" she asked, a bit higher in pitch than intended.

Josh finally lowered the intensity with which he had been regarding her. "Yes. I still write quite a bit, or maybe I should say that I have gone back to writing quite a bit."

Donna was much more comfortable in this conversation. "Your hobby was in abeyance?" She was unable to mask her pride in her word choice.

Josh apparently enjoyed it as well. "Well, you have been open about yourself, so I'll just give you enough information for you to understand what I meant when I said I was a different person now. As you know, I wrote a lot in high school. Though I had a very high opinion of my abilities, I soon learned that I was not nearly as creative, intelligent, or literate as I thought; I barely cut it in certain college courses. I guess it discouraged me, hurt my pride enough that I lost interest. Then I started dating the girl I thought was the love of my life. I'm not going to lie and say that I hadn't dated plenty of girls before her, but this one really had something over me."

Donna enjoyed the shyness with which he revealed himself to her.

"She was very negative regarding my ability to do anything, so with my interest in writing already a 1.5 on the 10-point scale, with her influence, it dropped below zero. Time went by, I got away from the hoe, and then, back on my own after our three years and near marriage, I went back to writing. First, I started thinking of writing and that lasted me about a year. Then, I was in Hong Kong, where I studied for several *long* months after graduating college, and an idea I had vaguely toyed with for years suddenly burst into my mind's eye, and I could not stop writing for anything. When I came home, I spent six months locked in my old room at my parents' house writing for hours a day, until, more than 500 pages later, my first novel was complete. That was five years ago, and though I go through dry spells, it has been going pretty steadily ever since."

"That's quite a summary," Donna said, not knowing where to begin questioning him further.

"Sort of," Josh said indifferently, seeming to doubt the importance of it. "I did use the phrase 'mind's eye,' however. I hate that phrase. I usually avoid it, but sometimes it fits so concisely."

"I hate 'brainchild,'" Donna stated, knowing exactly what he meant.

They shared a smile.

"Honestly, I think the weirdest thing that ever happened to me was that I came back from Hong Kong more grown up than when I left," he reflected, looking off to the side as though imagining scenes from his memory. "What's so weird is that it was nothing I planned for, and something I tried to deny, but it's true. It happened just like that. I lost all the arrogance, the need to prove myself, the need to impress others, all desire to do drugs or binge-drink. I felt above it all—not better than anyone else, but because I didn't care any more—I could not care any more."

Donna was fascinated by his candor and impressed by how he seemed to get so much closer to *real* in a few short months just by living life, without any intent or desire to do so.

"It makes me think of playing with dolls," Donna said wistfully.

"How so?" asked Josh with a quirky grin that clearly indicated he could not see where she was going.

"Just growing up, I mean. I used to love playing with dolls; generally, I played with babies and I was the mom, or with Barbies—I was just the omniscient force behind their dramas. I must have played until middle school, or so—much longer than most girls I knew—or at least, longer than most girls would admit. Anyway, now, when I try to play with a friend's child, it's as though I have forgotten how to play. I can't go back."

"That's exactly what it's like. I used to go to shows as often as I could afford, now I try to imagine myself at a concert, and I can't." He shrugged. "I still like the music, but going to a show just doesn't hold the interest that it once did. I don't think I'd know what to do with myself at one nowadays."

"Oh, God, I can't imagine it, either. What the hell would I do with myself? I would feel old and embarrassed. I mean, what if some sixteen-year-old kid asked me to buy him a beer? I would just die."

They both laughed out loud.

"I know I am still young, but I just don't know how to be it. In five years, I'll say, 'Why didn't I live a little more in my twenties? Now, I'm old, and that opportunity is gone.' Then, some odd number of years after that, I'll wonder again why I thought I was so old in my thirties, and why I didn't do more while I could have," Josh said, explaining the vicious cycle he felt himself sliding into at only twenty-six.

Thoughts of the future brought Donna's mind back around to Cameron. "It's been nice catching up," she began in a tone Josh had not expected, "but I think it's time for me to go home." She could not even look at him as she said it.

Though Josh's face fell, he understood she was not free to be out with him all night, though he had hoped she was going to decide differently.

"I need to go home and talk to Cameron. I don't think it's going to go particularly well, but I have never been through this before, so I can't really say what I expect."

Josh reached for her hand again, but Donna pulled away. "I can't pretend I don't want to see you again, but I also can't do it behind Cameron's back. I think cheating in any form is about the worst thing one person can do to another, and just being here with you makes me guilty of it. I couldn't possibly take this further without breaking it off with Cameron first." Donna's eyes moistened, but she did her best not to cry.

"I definitely respect that." Josh was sincere. "I'm sorry you have to go through something so hard. I guess it's one of those 'for the better' things, but who am I to judge?"

Donna sighed. It suddenly seemed impossible to keep her head up.

"Do you still want to exchange numbers? Maybe you can call me if you feel up to seeing me again." Their rapport had gone from easy to awkward so fast Josh was not even sure he still had a chance.

Donna nodded. "Yeah. It is a bit unpredictable right now, isn't it?"

Josh agreed, and they did as planned, Josh both writing down her number, and entering it into his phone. Nothing much was said until they parted at Donna's car. Josh did not even make a crack about how it had been parked the night before, and Donna had all but forgotten it had ever happened, the way a dream loses its composition the more wakeful the dreamer becomes.

Cameron was still playing his computer game when Donna reentered her apartment, feeling as though she was closing the door to a different world from the one she was entering. Her own home looked different. Darkness had crept in while she was out. Following the yellow light from the open door to the den, she felt as though she had fallen upon a scene from someone else's life. She and Cam had never fought, but she saw nothing but a fight transpiring in the next few minutes.

Donna did not speak, but lingered in the doorway until Cameron turned to her. "You weren't out long; did you have fun?"

Both aspects of his statement threw her, though she kept her emotion bottled up for as long as she could. She wondered how long was "long," when he had not even asked her where she was going, or when she was coming back. Then, to have the nerve to all but accuse her of having fun—like it had even been possible in all of her misery.

She shrugged noncommittally.

Cameron thought she looked tired. He got up, approaching her cautiously. "Donna?"

Donna refused to speak, knowing that as soon as she did, she would lose all composure. The hurt within her was not as tame as she had hoped, however, and it began forcing its way out through other avenues. Within a second or two, she was crying. It started out quiet and restrained, but eventually became all-consuming.

Cameron, dumbstruck by the display, hesitated before rushing toward her. She fought off his arms, which attempted to enfold her. Backing off, feeling the barrier that had flown up between them, Cameron felt on the verge of crying, as well.

Cameron's arms had been the first attribute Donna had ever loved about him. She felt safe and loved every time she was in them, and often demanded they be placed around her so she could revel in the tranquility they brought. Now, they were the only thing keeping her from finishing her insufferable task.

"Where were you?" Cameron croaked, suddenly realizing he had a reason to ask.

Donna stared at him, but words failed her. All she could do was cry. For Cameron, there was no longer a computer game, computer room, or apartment. It was as if they had entered a void.

He shook his head as though his dawning realization could be denied. "God! I thought you went out with Kenny or a girl from work, or something. I-I-I—" he stuttered.

"I can't believe I ever would have taken interest in someone else," Donna stammered painfully. "But I met someone I used to know for coffee."

Cameron's world was crashing down around him too loudly to hear clearly.

"I ran into him last night at the deli, when I thought you—"

Cameron's head turned sharply toward her with the speed of a psychopath snapping. "You met him when you thought I was dead, then you found out I was still alive, and went back to him?"

Donna cringed. She knew he would never hit her, but she still feared his hand; she had had the same experience with her very angry father on occasion as a child.

"Were you that desperate for an out? Did you wish I had died, so you could go on with your 'old friend'?" Cameron's tone was almost abusive. "Well, that's great! Here I am, feeling guilty as shit for something I not only had nothing to do with, but had been completely unaware of until you told me about it—and you're just like, 'Crap, I guess I still have to get married—not dead and all.'"

Her argument that he should have called her in the first place the night before was growing feebler by the instant. "I don't understand it, either. I have never been sincerely attracted to anyone but you before I saw Josh. Maybe I don't understand how relationships work. Maybe all of those people I felt I had defeated by finding my one and only, and not messing around with anything less beforehand, were all just ten years ahead of me."

Cameron raised his eyebrow. "This isn't that same Josh you always use as an example when we get into discussions about arrogant assholes, is it?"

Donna clammed up, looking shameful.

"What, he's changed now? He's had some kind of revelation; he was misunderstood back in high school when he was calling Kenny names and ignoring you? Now he thinks you're hot and wants to get in bed with you, you're going to let him because he was some kind of stud in high school that never looked twice at you—that never would have admitted to his friends he was into you because you weren't pretty enough to be seen with?" Cameron had finally berated her so badly that she had melted down the wall, sobbing with her whole body.

"I know those guys, too," he went on, not going to her. "Greg and Jay—my best buddies," he said with disdain. "That's who that guy is. You want to give up our future together for some fucking prick that's so full of himself he doesn't even care that he's breaking up an engagement just to get a notch on his bedpost? Well, that's fucking nice!"

Cameron finally backed away, still steaming, pacing the hall, unable to speak, filled with rage. Donna knew there was no defending Josh, even though she did not believe him on a par with Cameron's former buddies—certainly not the guy that Cameron had just described.

"What does Kenny think about all this?" Cameron finally asked, pausing to do so. "Does he even know? What's he gonna feel like when you want him to hang out with the asshole who made his life *miserable* all those years? Are you just gonna take him off like an old pair of panties, too? Or, maybe now that Kenny's not gay, he's an acceptable member of the Josh crowd as well?"

"Stop it," Donna squeaked.

Cameron finally realized that he was all but spitting and had reduced Donna to a puddle on the floor. His tears then were of shame for the way he had treated her, for the way he had not thought himself capable of treating her. He knelt beside her, taking her hand. As she looked up at him, the fear in her eyes stabbed his heart like a dagger.

"I can't believe I am losing you. I can't believe the girl I felt so secure with could want to be with someone else. Believe it or not, I do understand what you are feeling. You doubt the strength of our bond because a challenger persuaded you to fold in on it. Your lack of experience in relationships brought you to this point; you just have to decide which path to take. If you need more information, I have to let you gather it." He shrugged, resigned. "I am not, however, calling him a threat. A challenge can be met and conquered, a threat requires defensive force to overcome, and I do not believe that is where we're at."

Donna found herself so stunned by his sagacity that she almost forgot Josh right there, but the little thing in the back of her mind that told her it would never forget about Josh, even after she and Cam were married, took dominance.

"I am a *real* person with real feelings," Cameron began again, using another face of the *real* coinage, one that reinforced the fact that he existed and his feelings were valid. "If I mean the vows I still intend to say to you on our wedding day, I have to respect your curiosity and the fact that this is something you need to do before you are ready to say your vows to me." He spoke with confidence that their marriage plans were not terminated. "If I am wrong, I don't get you, and that's not a bet I would be willing to make unless I was a hundred percent certain I would win."

Part of Donna hoped he was right because it would make everything so nice if it were true. Another part found his willingness to let her go a sign that perhaps breaking up was the right thing to do. Cameron read the thought in her face.

"I don't want you to think I am okay with this, that I am going to let you go, bake some cookies, go to bed, then expect to wake up with you saying you could not believe you ever doubted us, and we should get married that day because everything is all poodles and lampshades."

Donna looked at him the same way she had looked at her grandfather the time he had claimed, upon entering a chic dining establishment her family had tried to drag him to, "It's darker than a bag of assholes in here."

Cameron caught the look, but did not stop his defense. "I would rather lose you professing my love to you than let you go questioning the ease with which I did it. I am in agony knowing that I will be without you for a time. I can put up with it, though, if it means you'll feel reassured when you come back to me; I'll keep your wedding band sparkling until you do."

Donna did not think she could hurt so much, but somehow this grief was harder to bear than Cameron's death, as this had been brought on by her own selfishness. Not even Josh could share the blame.

There was nothing much said after that. There was a lot of crying and hugging, and just a little kiss on Donna's head as Cameron walked out after gathering his things and headed home to his parents' for however long he would have to wait for his bride.

Donna sank onto a bar stool at her kitchen counter after Cameron left. Part of her hoped he would come back, that it would be as though he had never decided to leave, but after a long minute, she knew he would not be doing so, and after eight more, Donna finally put her head down on the bar, giving up completely. She did not cry this time. It seemed she was out of tears. Her eyes were sore, and she had never felt so "there" before. The countertop was cool, providing a feeling similar to that of the bathroom floor after a long stint of puking. Her eyes slowly began to close.

She was startled out of her doze by the house phone ringing just inches from her ear. She glanced at the caller ID before answering.

"Hey, Kenny," she said sleepily.

"Did I wake you?"

"I don't know," Donna sighed heavily.

"I just wanted to check on you. Things were insane this morning, and I hoped they had simmered down a little."

"They have." She sounded closed and emotionless.

"Well, I can see that you're not in the mood to talk, but we should do coffee or lunch tomorrow, okay?"

"Yeah." Donna gave a drawn-out yawn.

"Okay, sweetie. I'll call you in the morning—not too early, I promise."

Donna nodded, and Kenny hung up.

Donna half-wished she had not deceived Kenny, but she was in no mood to go over it all again so soon. It was easier for Kenny to think she and Cameron had made up. Plus, she knew she could not explain her meeting with Josh without a flimsy excuse that she did not feel she had the strength to uphold.

The phone call gave her an idea, though. She reached into her purse and dug out her cell phone. Finding Josh's number in her address book, she selected it and waited for the connection.

She felt like a giddy high school girl calling the popular boy for the first time.

"Hi," Josh said as if he knew it was her.

"Hi."

"Everything okay?" he asked.

"No," she said. "It actually sucks quite a bit."

Josh was not sure of the status of their relationship yet, and was hesitant to respond.

Donna relieved his nerves. "I'm not looking for a shoulder to cry on or anything. Kenny would be here for that. I just want to get out of my apartment and have some fun. I discovered a few minutes ago that I am out of tears, and there's no point in being sad if I can't get a good cry out of it."

Josh laughed, more relaxed. "I think I can help you with that."

"Well, we already went out for coffee today, so I guess now we have to just booze it up."

"I think you're right. I happen to have a pretty full bar at my place. At the risk of sounding like a total jerk, why don't we get totally trashed? You can stay over. I have two separate beds, and it's not an attempt to—"

"I'd love to," Donna cut him off.

"Besides, if you drive home after all of the alcohol I intend to serve you, you might end up parked in a planter somewhere."

Donna laughed heartily for the first time since she had last been with him. "Hey, I wasn't drunk; I was distraught."

"Mm-hmm," he muttered incredulously.

"Whatever—where do you live?" Her voice came out a bit squeaky.

Donna was at Josh's apartment in less than ten minutes. She felt almost scandalous as she walked up to the door. Across the parking lot, someone glanced her way, and she felt *obvious*, taking a little jump as she quickened her pace. Her butterflies increased threefold when Josh opened the door a moment later. It was odd for her to feel so intensely; even in the first days of her relationship with Cameron, she had never felt so nervous.

Josh welcomed her politely to his home, showed her around the first floor, and motioned for her to have a seat in the living room.

"All right. I believe I promised you booze." He rubbed his hands together. "What's your poison?"

Donna laughed. "I feel compelled to say vodka, but it's actually gin."

Josh grinned, proud of his cleverness; Donna having understood his Breakfast Club reference.

"Tonic and lime?"

"Of course."

"Coming right up," Josh said, handing her the remote and going to the kitchen to make her drink.

Donna turned the TV on and began flipping through the channels, still undecided by the time he placed her drink, garnished with a lime wedge and a little black straw. He had even served it in a short glass with a flared edge, on a plum-colored cocktail napkin.

"Fancy," she commented, impressed.

"Presentation is half the enjoyment." He said, mocking the old G.I. Joe slogan, 'knowing is half the battle.'

She found him charming. Catching herself staring a little too long, she went back to surfing the channels. "There's never anything on."

"I know. Let's just put something on for background noise. We'll probably not pay much attention to it, anyway."

Donna handed the remote back to him. "Anything but news. I hate news of any kind."

"Me, too. It's always so depressing. I'd rather just not know."

"I am exactly the same way. Ignorance *is* bliss. I only ever know what's going on if it's so major there's no avoiding it or if I happen to hear it on morning radio."

"I bet you don't vote, either."

Donna smiled sheepishly.

"It's okay, neither do I."

"I just don't feel like I have solid opinions on the issues, so I figure one less uneducated vote is better than closing my eyes and jabbing at something. The only point of doing that is to say you voted." Donna shrugged. "I think I would vote if I really believed in an issue, or were really opposed to it."

"I know. It's such a stigma—'the non-voter'—but like you said, why add a draw-by-numbers Scantron to all the real votes?" Josh took a sip of his beer.

After a few minutes, Donna slurped the last drops against the ice in the bottom of her glass.

"Hey, little fish," Josh smiled. "Do you want another, or do we need to pace you?"

"I'll start pacing after the next one," Donna promised.

This time, Donna followed him into the kitchen, dawdling as she stopped to look at pictures, knickknacks, and the like. As she made her way to the fridge, she noticed that he had poetry magnets scattered all over its front. She read a few of the lines he had constructed, laughing a bit.

"Those things are lame, I know, but sometimes it's fun," Josh said, wishing he had had the forethought to hide them before she came over.

"They used to have them on cookie trays in the lobby of the student health care facility at U of A," Donna commented, absently reorganizing some of the magnets.

"I don't remember the last time I played with them, to tell the truth." Josh shrugged as he slid her concoction toward her.

Hearing the glass moving across the kitchen island, Donna turned around, caught the glass, and avoided his closeness by bringing it to her lips, and taking a sip. "Kenny and I have a kind of game we play, if you can call it a game; it starts out kinda funny, then drives you insane when you can't stop doing it any more, no matter how hard you try."

"What's that?" Josh backed off a little.

"You choose two letters, like PT, for example, and then you keep coming up with PT things—like 'plum tomato,' for instance—until someone can't come up with one. The problem is, you can always come up with another one, and once your mind starts working in that pattern of thought, it's really hard to break it. So, the next day there are like ten of them instantly in your mind when you wake up, and then a week later you still keep catching yourself coming up with them. I tell you, it's a horrible commitment to make to get started on it.."

"What ever made you come up with that?"

"We were trying to think of the name of a band, and Kenny swore it started with a D. We kept spouting off D words, trying to stumble onto it through serendipity, if that's possible; then, once we decided we weren't going to figure it out, we tried to stop saying D words and couldn't—even when we thought we had exhausted our combined vocabulary—they just kept coming."

Josh was laughing pretty hard, taking in her idiosyncrasies as he watched her explain. "So, then it got to be two letters somehow?"

"I was going to physical therapy a couple years ago, and one day Kenny asked if I was 'PT-ing it' that day. Even though I always called it that, I couldn't for the life of me think of what he meant by it. I was like, 'Potty training?' and he was like, 'No, pregnant teacher,' referring to that old joke from grade school."

"What joke?"

"You didn't have that joke?" Donna cried a little too boisterously.

Josh shook his head, stunned by her expressive demeanor, but happy to be witnessing it.

"You have to know it! It's from, like, third grade, where one kid asks, 'Are you PT?' then if the other kid says, 'Yes,' the first one laughs and says, 'Ha ha you're a pregnant teacher.' If the second kid says, 'No,' the first kid laughs and says, 'Ha ha, you're not potty trained.' It's a catch-22."

"Wow," said Josh, not sure how take it.

Donna's face was flushed. She set down her drink, thinking she ought to be embarrassed, but not feeling that way.

"Maybe I should start pacing myself now," she suggested.

"Wanna sit outside? We should take advantage of the one week in spring when it's not too cold or too hot."

Donna agreed eagerly and followed him out through the glass doors.

The crisp night air was almost sobering. "It's nice out here," Donna said, looking around, wide-eyed. "You have so many trees. It almost feels like we're not in the city any more."

"I know. That's one reason I chose this place. I like the desert; it can be beautiful, but I think people have an inherent fondness of trees, grass, and plants—like we know they provide the oxygen we need, so we like to be around them." He looked around, as though also examining the place for the first time.

"You still can't see the stars, though," Donna said sadly, squinting at the sky as though she would see them if she tried hard enough.

"No. His hair remains hidden behind the city lights."

Josh had a big grin on his face when Donna looked at him. "I don't know why you like that poem so much," she blushed. "I recently heard a fashion commentator say that the Goth look should stay among depressed teenagers who write bad poetry. That's my tenth grade in a nutshell."

"That's why it's so great. It is the essence of you at that time in your life." He had regained the intuitive look he wore at their meeting the night before. "No, don't discredit me here," he said in response to her sardonic expression. "I'm being honest—just like you were when you wrote that poem. I mean, think about it. Do you think now you could so accurately put your fifteen-year-old spirit into a poem? Don't you see that though you could never recapture that moment, it is so vividly detailed in those few lines, that you can almost relive it by reciting them?"

Donna was, at first, a bit taken aback by how passionate he was about the poem, but then reminded herself that it was writing he was passionate about, not just her poem.

"That is why I said you are my muse. I have stumbled across that poem about three or four times in the ten years since it was put in our poetry notebook. Each time, it struck me harder, until I finally realized that the poem captured the quintessence of you at that time. It's one of those things that you can only realize with age. I told you that I am at the deli all the time, writing. I have several completed novels, but as I plan them, I sometimes have to wait on a certain idea—like I can tell that I won't be able to write it until I have lived a little more, until I have become what I want to write."

Donna was impressed. Somehow, she had gone from explaining nonsense games to being exemplified as a poetic intellect. She shrugged. "Well, it does make sense. I mean, I heard that now all the kids are going Emo. I am so out of touch with that age group that I don't even really know what it means. A girl at work kind of briefed me on it."

"I don't really know what it is either, but it's better than the terrible hair out there lately. The shaggy look was huge in Asia when I was in Hong Kong, and it looked just as terrible there as it does here. What's worse is that here it seems there are more curly-haired guys, which gives their 'fro even more Chia Pet-like ability."

Donna shot out a quick huff of laughter that developed into an aggressive hiccup.

"You alright there, sport?" Josh leaned into her, patting her back surreptitiously.

Donna rolled her eyes at him. "I'm fine. I was just thinking about that poem. I don't know if you ever saw my grade, but I remember going over it with Ms. Thompson. She refused to give me an A because she disapproved of my use of 'Gothic' as a noun. She would not accept that people used it in that context all the time. I refused to deny the term, so I got a B-. All this after she taught us about creating and bending meaning, and how each generation redefines the words that apply to them."

"That only proves my point further. Your use of the word 'Gothic' after being told you couldn't use it was an act of defiance, otherwise called rebellion, otherwise known as the agenda of most teenagers."

"I suppose it was," Donna sighed, looking back to the expanse of stars. "You know, in Tucson, the street lights are dim yellow—at least, around the university they are. I don't know if it's true—it makes sense since there is an observatory on campus—but someone once told me they were like that to maximize the visibility of the stars."

Josh sent his gaze upward, too. "I think they verified the tenth planet's existence recently. I don't know much about it, since I don't really seek out news of any kind, but it's kind of cool to think maybe we have proven there is more out there than we have believed for so long. It's one for the Darwinists, anyway."

"I wonder what they will call it. We were just talking about how generations redefine terms. Do you think the namers will continue in the Roman tradition, or will they give it a name that more clearly defines our times?"

"Maybe NASA has rules for planets, like the school district does for elementary schools—they must be named for a Native American people, whereas a planet must be named according to Roman Mythology, except maybe Earth. I don't know if it's Roman or not," he said, fearing that he had just sounded like a complete idiot.

"As long as it's not something ridiculous, or a normal sounding name with a weird spelling so that no one will ever get it right. We have enough of that going on down here." Donna made a sound in her throat to indicate her disgust with that particular national contagion.

"You know what's funny, though? No matter how bad a name is, if you like a person with that name, or if you hear it enough, it grows on you and can even become one of your favorites," Josh noted, sinking into his plastic lounge chair. "The reverse is also true; like, if you always liked a name, then you meet somebody with it whom you can't stand, you begin to hate it. It's like the chicken and the egg—does the name define the person, or the person the name?"

"Neither," Donna said grimly, reflecting on her own experience. "My name is Donna, which means 'beautiful woman.' I am not beautiful because I am named Donna, and my name was not fated to be Donna to match myself, as I am not beautiful."

"You're not?" Josh asked, leaning toward her with large, sad eyes.

Donna looked hard at him, trying to find any hint of sarcasm in his visage, but she could not. He kept his gaze steady upon her.

She half-smiled. "You are getting dangerous," she warned him, hoping she sounded more playful than accusatory.

Josh's eyes released her, and he apologized with his head bowed slightly. "I'm sorry. I know I said there would be none of that. I just got a little caught up in the moment."

"It's okay," Donna assured him, patting his back gently. "Maybe it's the atmosphere. We should get back in. I gotta pee, anyway."

"Well, that's one way to kill the mood—pull the plug right out of the wall."

She slapped him playfully on the shoulder. "Where's the can, then?"

Laughing, Josh replied, "It's straight ahead once you get to the top of the stairs."

"Stairs?" Donna whined.

"It's a short flight, I promise. I'll refresh your beverage while you're up."

"All right," Donna groaned, dragging herself into the apartment, across the living room, and stomping up the stairs.

Josh laughed as she went, but knew he was going to have to lighten up, or his emotions would get him into trouble.

Donna came back a couple minutes later to another perfect gin and tonic and greeted it with a good quaff.

"Do you play cards at all?" Josh asked, indicating the deck he had set out in her absence.

With a big smile on her face, she raised her glass and gave it an emphatic wiggle, hoping her underarm fat did not waddle too much, thanking herself for keeping up with the pushups against the counter she had been doing on nearly every bathroom trip for the last two months. "Again, gin is my poison."

"A favorite of mine, as well."

At first, Donna's score columns were nice and neat, but by the time her third gin and tonic was drained, the numbers had become a sloppy scrawl, impossibly still intelligible to her.

On the deciding hand, after they had been neck and neck most of the way through, Josh ginned when Donna only needed one more card to do so herself. She upturned his discard, and just as she had predicted to herself, it was the one she needed.

"Fat Judy!" she cried as she slammed the card back on top of the pile.

"What?" Josh actually spit out a bit of beer upon hearing it.

"It's just an expression," Donna said, joining in with his laughter.

"No, it's not," he argued.

"I mean, it's an inside joke between Kenny and me. One time when we were around his mom, I almost shouted, 'Fuck!' but I knew we'd get in trouble, so at the last minute, I turned it into whatever I could think of that started with Fff--."

Josh was laughing hysterically.

"It's still pretty funny, though, I guess." Donna almost started laughing again.

"Sorry, it was just so unexpected." Josh straightened up. "I hope his mom isn't named Judy."

"No. Thank God. I guess if she had been it would have been worse than an F-bomb." Donna smiled to herself. "I have always felt guilty saying it, though. I mean, I know the meaning is arbitrary; it's just based on how the words sound together, but I am still afraid to offend people who try to glean false meaning from it. Especially now that I am thinner, I don't want someone who doesn't know I have been fat and gone through all that goes with it thinking I am demeaning them."

"You tend to overanalyze your self-image, don't you?"

"Sort of. Physical characteristics—yes; personality—not so much."

Josh obviously felt bad for her. Donna did not want this to become a sob fest, so she let her heavy head roll a bit, as though her neck could no longer support its weight, then told Josh that if he did not show her to a bed right now, he would be carrying her to one later.

Donna did have one last silly fit as she stopped midway up the stairs and continued the rest of the way up on her hands and knees. She made a triumphant effort to get semi-upright again for her two-yard walk down the hall, through the bedroom door, and over to the bed, which Josh turned down for her. Donna hit her knee on the front of the daybed before crawling into it.

"Do you want some pajama pants or anything?" Josh asked kindly.

"No," Donna said, sounding as though she was practically asleep already.

"Goodnight, little fish." Josh smiled lovingly as he covered her up, knowing she would not be responding.

Before going to his own room, he placed three tablets and a large glass of water on her bedside table, watching her lying there, out cold, looking oddly like a little girl after a long day.

The next morning, when Donna woke, she knew she was somewhere unfamiliar before she even opened her eyes. She felt happy to be there, and though she had at some point woken up enough to take her medicine and drink some water, she had not realized that she was sharing a room with Josh's computer. The door to her room was only partially closed, but she listened for signs as to whether or not Josh was awake. After a good moment, she got up to go to the bathroom.

Though she was groggy, Donna was glad to find that she did not have much of a hangover as she stood there examining herself in the mirror. She wished she had removed her make-up the night before, but had to admit that even if she had brought cleanser, she would not have been able to apply it in her state. Her contacts stuck slightly, but were not too dry to be irritating, and she was glad that she had worn such comfy clothes, as she did not even feel as though she had been sleeping in them all night.

When she left the bathroom a moment later, feeling guilty for not doing any push-ups while in there, she finally heard sounds of Josh rustling about downstairs. He had left his bedroom door open, and Donna took a quick peek in before joining him on the ground level.

"Hey, there," Josh greeted her jauntily. "You're an early riser, too?"

Donna noticed on the microwave clock that it was not much past 8:30 a.m.

"Yeah. I used to sleep all day when I was up late, but now it doesn't matter when I go to bed; I never get up too late, especially after drinking. Though around 11:30 or so, I will probably be ready to crash for a nap."

"Speaking of drinking, how you doin'?" He leaned casually on the kitchen island, giving her an 'I know what you did last night' look.

"I'm good actually," Donna said truthfully, though her voice sounded weak.

"I'm glad. I was a little worried the way you went out so fast. Did you take the tablets I left you?"

"Yes, thanks. I must have noticed them there some time in the night."

Josh began laughing. "Do you remember how you got up the stairs last night?"

Donna gave him an apprehensive look.

"You crawled up on all fours, saying it was too much work."

Donna laughed a bit guiltily.

"And I have something to thank you for!" he said, not sounding thankful at all.

"What?" Donna asked, in a cute little voice that did not hide her fear of what it might be.

Josh picked up a pad of paper from the counter behind him and began reading.

"Prehensile Tail, Published Tome, Piano Teacher, Prize Turnip, Pimply Teenager, Party Time, Piping Tunes, Pizza Topping, Peeping Tom, Possibly Twisted—" he said the last one with a meaningful look at her.

"No!" Donna cried, covering her ears. "Don't start it."

"It's too late," Josh said in a futile tone. "I woke up with it, and now I can't shut it off."

"Crap. Why'd I have to ramble on about that?" Donna cursed herself.

"Well, do you want to go get some breakfast? I'm cool with anything: fast food, bagels, sit down—"

Donna's tummy rumble answered for her. "Plainly tacit."

"I must be the biggest dork if flirting with wordplay is this sexy to me," Josh admitted.

Donna smiled.

They eventually decided to get bagels, but not at the deli where they had already been seen twice together in such a short amount of time. Donna did not go back inside with him after they arrived at his complex, but said her goodbye in the parking lot. She found it hard to leave, but felt that it would be harder to stay. Her mind was drifting back to Cameron more often than she felt comfortable for it to do while she was still in Josh's company.

Josh already felt lonely by the time he entered his apartment. He knew if he was not there already, he was at least beginning to fall in love with Donna. She was fun, and the two of them had so much in common that he wondered how he could have been such a jerk in high school not to see it then. He felt undeserving of her, but fervidly hoped they would continue to get along so fondly.

As he went by the fridge to collect a few bottle caps to throw in the trash, he noticed a message arranged on the refrigerator door that he had not composed himself. "Death and Poetry." It read like a title. It was striking—just three little, common words, yet they affected him somehow.

There is a saying in cards that, though it had always been familiar to Donna, as her extended family were big card game aficionados, had shown another nuance of meaning to her as an older teenager. *Thin to win.* In cards, it referred to cutting the deck into one thin stack and one thick stack, instead of two equal ones, in hopes of bringing luck to the one cutting. Donna later realized that it bore heavily upon other aspects of life, as well.

In her view of the world, another concept also stood out. *Thin and pretty.* This could be broken down to the supposition that achieving one would entail attaining the other. Donna, never believing that she was pretty, or would ever be pretty, did somewhere in the back of her mind feel that she could be thin, or at least thinner, and then, by some divine intervention, she would also become pretty—or at least prettier. Logic told her that the concept was absurd, but nevertheless, the two attributes seemed intertwined. In fact, it often seemed to Donna that thin people's lives were perfect. They were pretty and happy, and people wanted to be in their company.

When Donna became thin, however, glamour did not come along as part of a packaged deal. While she was pretty good for an average Jane, she still needed to lose about ten pounds to reach the high end of the Hollywood starlet weight range. But even she, who was her toughest critic, could not deny the success she had made; especially as she noted the difference in the area around her when she sat in a chair or lay in a tub. The slimming of her face had helped tremendously in her pursuit of miraculous beauty, but nothing extravagant had come of it. Generally, she still felt like the monstrosity that had looked back at her in the mirror over fifty pounds ago.

She sincerely believed it was impossible for anyone but the toadiest of lechers to ever find her attractive. Though she had improved quite a bit, it would never be enough to satisfy her.

6

When Donna came home to her own apartment, she felt the late-morning need for a nap coming on, just as she had predicted it would. She was glad, too. It meant she could avoid, at least for an hour or two, reflection on the weekend thus far. It was hard to believe it had only been a weekend; it felt as though her whole life had changed.

When, at last, Donna could not squeeze another five-minute nod into her nap, she conceded to getting up. The message light on her phone was blinking, but she was not hopeful that it was Cameron, and was a little afraid it was Josh. It turned out to be Kenny, reminding her that she had promised him lunch or coffee. Donna had been a little downhearted that it had not been Cameron, but until that moment, calling him had been the last thing on her mind, so she could not really blame him. It was not that she did not care where he was or what he was up to, but she could not ration another percentage of her brainpower on it when it was already at capacity with everything else. Plus, she had to have as much strength as possible to have an intelligible conversation with Kenny, as there was no denying what their meeting was going to turn into, no matter how they tried to avoid it. It would be like going out with work friends on the weekend. No matter how far off topic it is in the beginning, the subject matter always comes back around to work—there is no escaping it. Knowing that, Donna preferred being strong enough to lead in with it, rather than having it turned around on her. Therefore, their meeting had to be a lunch. Coffee was really more for gossip or catch-up.

They met at a place Donna knew had slow service, ensuring they would have plenty of time to talk. As soon as they were seated, Donna dove into it. "So, I'm sure you weren't fooled last night, but yes, I lied to you. Things are not fine; Cameron and I separated."

"What?" Kenny was caught off guard.

"Like you believed me?" Donna scoffed.

"Well, no, but I was going to let you say so as long as you needed." He shrugged. "I guess you don't need to."

"I guess not." Donna shrugged, too, feeling good about being open with someone other than Cameron or Josh. "I was just tired and not ready to talk about it, you know?"

"So, how'd it leave off with Cameron?" he probed softly.

Donna took a moment. "Not well. I had never seen him angry before, but it was weird because he calmed down almost instantly and made the whole thing very amicable. He left for his parents' house around ten, and I haven't seen him since." She threw her hands up.

"Wow, so he had totally just left when I called—no wonder you weren't in the mood."

"Yeah. It was a weird day. In the morning, I was all pissed at him for being alive, then understanding and forgiving—if you can call it that, though he really was not the one who needed it—then we didn't talk all day. There was just this—" she took a moment to describe it. "Palpable tension," she managed to say before fits of laughter exploded from her.

Kenny did not even need to ask. "Don't tell me you reopened Pandora's Box."

"I never should have told Josh about that, he's the one—"

Kenny's look cut her off before his words could. "You told Josh about the PT game? When did this happen?"

Donna sobered and looked like she could crawl under the table right then, like Kenny had once done when a boy he liked entered a restaurant they were at when he thought he was having a bad hair day.

"I actually saw him twice last night," Donna came clean. "We went to coffee after I ate dinner, then I came home, broke up with Cameron, and went back to hang out at his place all night."

"Naughty," Kenny commented with relish, fishing for more.

"Not that naughty," she assured him. "We actually had a really nice time."

"Ew! Is that where you answered my call?" He looked dishonored.

"Of course not. It was after your call that I called him to forget about everything."

"Wait a minute. Josh Addington—the same guy we used as an icon of our most hated personality just two days ago. That's you'd rather have cheer you up?"

"He's not the same guy we were talking about, and I really like him."

Kenny was appalled. "You can't be serious."

"I am. I actually think you guys would get along well, too, if it was possible for you to get beyond the past."

Kenny's jaw dropped just as the waitress came to take their drink order. As soon as she left, he went into it. "You have this awesome guy in Cameron, and you dump him for a former punk that you only met for a few minutes and decided is a changed man?"

Donna put up a hand to stop him. "I am already familiar with this side of the story. I got enough of it from Cameron."

Kenny had not meant to hurt her. "I'm sorry, Donna. I'm just afraid of what you're walking out on."

Donna nodded, accepting his apology. "Look, I don't think it's right, either, but I have to figure it out before I get married. I don't want to wind up divorced in a few years, like everybody else." She reiterated for the second time in two days.

Kenny kept silent, maintaining his sympathy, but not offering false hope.

"I wish we could just go back to the MistaSista and Donna days," Donna groaned nostalgically. "Why didn't I have a stage name again, by the way?"

Kenny smiled, looking embarrassed. "You weren't 'fabulous' enough for one."

"Well, you were just fabulous enough for the both of us, I guess, because recording those shows was the most fun I can remember having."

He blushed.

"Until I began falling in love with Cameron."

"There's your answer," Kenny said. "You love Cameron, so go get him back. End it with Josh before you do something unforgivable."

Donna looked, if possible, even more morose than she had. "I wish I could. Even though I long for Cameron, I can't just end it with Josh. I will never be able to fully commit to Cameron if I am always curious about Josh. Then I wonder—what if it's not Josh, per se? What if it's just the allure of being with someone else? I have never dated anyone but Cameron, ever. Maybe he gave me the confidence I needed to date. Maybe, I don't really love Cameron the way a wife should love a husband; maybe we're just compatible."

"Well, you're not being very compatible right now. You seem more like lovers in a rut than two previously compatible people," Kenny interjected.

Donna shrugged.

"Look, Josh may be a changed person. I'll admit I don't know, but you don't know him yet, either. What if in two weeks you realize you gave up your fiancé for a nowhere relationship with someone you're already growing out of?"

"You can't fight feeling with logic—it's like trying to fight devout faith with the theory of evolution. It's moot. Or *mood*, I suppose."

"I give up then. There's nothing you can do but keep pursuing Josh—or whatever it is you are chasing."

"It's the only conclusion I come to also, and Cameron said so, too." She frowned. "It's just weird. I can't decide if I'm cheating. I mean, I am technically not with Cameron as of last night, but we were engaged—can it really just end like that? Plus, the whole reason it happened was because I told him that I was interested in Josh. I admit that cheating doesn't require sex—which Josh and I are nowhere near right now, but I think I was doing it just meeting him for coffee before Cameron and I had even had words."

Donna looked to Kenny for his opinion.

"It's a tough situation," he commented lamely.

"Really?" Donna snorted mordantly.

"You can unscrew a bottle cap, but not a person." He looked at her with stern implication.

"See!" Donna cried. "That's the MistaSista I was missing! I would have preferred snapping and neck jerking, but I understand that your more animated days are behind you."

Kenny smiled, unable to keep a serious front.

"You're still gay where it counts. Whatever you do with women behind closed doors is your own business."

Kenny regained his sincerity a moment after pretending he was bored with the gay/ not gay comments. "I just don't want to see you end up with some male version of Tianna—stuck because you don't know what else to do."

"I hardly think—" Donna began heavily.

"I don't mean Josh—just in general." Kenny saved her the spiel. "Look, you can't deny your confusion, and I can't deny the knowledge. As much as I hate to sit back and watch this thing play out, I don't have a choice."

Donna shook her head. "How did I ever wind up on *this* side of the table?"

Kenny did not fully grasp her meaning.

"What you just said is exactly how I felt about your little whirl with Tianna." She rolled her eyes. "Only you are wondering how I could be away from Cameron, and I was wondering how you could be with Tianna."

"Learn from my experience then," Kenny suggested emphatically. "Don't put yourself in the same kind of fix with Josh. Skip to the part where I was right, and you reunite with Cameron."

"If only it was that easy. Tianna was clearly a nasty bitch. If Josh is still the asshole he was in high school, it hasn't come out yet."

"Just don't sleep with him."

"Kenny, I just told you—"

"It's not that easy to plan. Just don't do something you can't take back. As long as Cameron is on the backburner, don't destroy every path back to him."

"You're not regretting that you were with Tianna?"

"No—you're on the telling side, and I'm on the listening/advising side, remember?"

Donna was too sickened by how she felt to retort again; the guilt she had brought with her had begun to churn in her stomach.

Kenny finally relinquished his hold. "So, do you still want to eat?"

"I want a huge, greasy cheeseburger with extra mayonnaise and chili-cheese fries." Donna demanded as though she had been planning it for a month.

"You know you'll hate yourself later," Kenny warned.

"I hate myself now," Donna whined, though a smile broke across her features.

Kenny shook his head, knowing his logic had been defeated, but never desiring to abandon his best friend.

Donna was at Josh's place the next Tuesday night. She took Monday to let things settle, and to reflect, but all day at work on Tuesday, Donna could think of nothing else but her next encounter with him. Their rapport had not changed much since last time she was there, but it was, perhaps, a little toned down, as there had been no alcohol involved They did play games again, though. As Cameron was generally disinclined to play Scrabble and usually half-assed it when he did cave in and play, Donna was glad to have the chance to play it with a word buff.

Her cell phone rang just as she completed a high-scoring word.

"I'm sorry, I normally would ignore it, but it's my mom's ring; do you mind?"

Josh shooed her toward the direction of her purse. "I'll still be counting your points when you get back."

Donna was laughing as she picked up the phone. "Hey," she said casually, trying to straighten her tone.

"Hi." Donna's mother also sounded in high spirits. "I just parked; how much longer do you think you're gonna be?"

Donna was caught completely by surprise. She tried to remember where she was apparently supposed to be, but kept drawing a blank. "I'm not sure."

"Well, I'm gonna go in and look around, so just call me when you get to the store, and I'll come to the front."

Donna clapped a hand to her head so hard it hurt. "Oh, my god!" she could not stop from crying out.

Josh looked at her in alarm, but she waved at him to let him know there was no emergency.

"What's the matter?" her mom asked, sounding worried.

"Mom, I'm so sorry. I feel terrible, but I thought the dress-shopping thing was on Thursday. I'm with Kenny on the other side of town."

Donna's mom made a sound of indignation. "Donna, I drove all the way out here," she whined, practically singing her daughter's name as she groaned.

"I'm so sorry, Mom. I feel terrible. I can totally be there in about forty-five minutes," she said desperately, though her desperation was for her desire not to go, rather than guilt for missing the date.

"No, no. Do whatever it is you are doing." Her mother replied. "I am gonna look a tad since I'm here, but we'll go together another time."

Donna thought her mom was fighting back tears, and it broke her heart to deceive her. "I feel like the biggest jerk."

"No, honey. Just forget it. We'll reschedule, but Thursday doesn't work for me, so why don't I just call you back tomorrow about it. Run along back to your friend."

"Okay. Bye, Mom," Donna said with great difficulty.

Her mom did not reply before hanging up.

Donna took a moment before facing Josh, who had come over to put his arms around her. She wished she could refuse them, but she could not. She knew she should never be in the arms of anyone but Cameron, but there she was.

"I can't believe I lied to her like that," Donna sniffed, looking up at him, trying hard not to cry.

"Well, until you tell her what happened between you and Cameron, there isn't really a way to explain why you couldn't go, or who you were with," Josh sympathized.

"That reminds me—I need to call Kenny real quick," Donna said, turning back to her phone and choosing his number. "God, I feel like I'm fifteen. Hey, Kenny," Donna said in a hurried voice when he answered. "I know this is totally lame, and there's only a very slim chance that this might come up, but if my mom ever mentions anything, will you agree that you and I were hanging out tonight, though she and I were supposed to have gone dress shopping?"

"You're with Josh?"

"Uh-huh."

Kenny sighed. "Okay, but you can't hide the 'no wedding' thing forever."

"I know. Thanks."

"Talk to you later," Kenny answered, and hung up, knowing that she was not hanging around to chat.

"God, this feels like shit," Donna said, seating herself carefully on the back of the couch.

Josh took her hand. "I'm sorry, Donna. I hate that you feel that way because of me."

"Don't say that," Donna insisted. "It was my choice to meet you at the deli, even after I knew Cameron was safe and sound."

An awkward silence ensued, though it did not last long.

"I don't suppose you still feel like letting me have a chance to catch up?" Josh finally asked, eyeing the game board.

"No, it's okay. I don't want to leave, I just feel like I could use a drink." Donna smiled coyly.

"I know just how you like it." Josh smiled, glad that she was not leaving. "Believe it or not, you didn't clean me out of gin last time."

"Tall, please." Donna smiled. It felt better being with a friend than being all alone.

When he handed her the finished product, she held it up and said, "Here's to you catching up!" Then she took about half of it in one chug.

Donna dreaded the telephone call her mother had promised to make the next day. Even when the phone rang with her parents' home number on the caller ID display, Donna was unsure of exactly what she was going to say.

"This is Donna." She always answered in a professional tone—'just in case.'

"Hi, it's Mom," Marlene DiSimone replied much more cheerily than Donna had expected.

"Look, about last night," Donna began, "about me being with Kenny, you see—"

Donna's mom stopped her. "It's okay. I don't mind that you got the days wrong. I know you probably had a lot on your mind. It's important that you are there for your *friends*," she emphasized the word oddly. "There will be plenty of time for dress shopping."

Donna felt her surroundings disappear. She heard nothing but her drumming heart and buzzing head. Her vision seemed arbitrary. Had her mom heard about Josh, but if so, why was she so happy? Kenny and Cameron were the only ones who could tell.

"I guess," Donna tried to recover, "but I still feel—"

"I know, you still dislike the fact that you forgot about it; but really, it's okay," Marlene sighed as though it was a precursor to an announcement she would rather not make. "The truth is I ran into Belinda George at the mall this morning. It's been years since we've talked, so we did a little shopping and caught up."

Donna saw where this was going. Kenny's mom, Belinda, must have told her mom about Kenny's recent pronouncement, which made Marlene think Donna had been so involved with consoling Kenny that she had forgotten about her own life.

"I see," said Donna, not getting too comfortable too fast. "She told you that Kenny's a little different than she thought he was?"

"Yes, and I think it's great!" Marlene squealed, unable to contain herself, though Donna did not quite understand why.

Her forehead wrinkled as she asked, her tone clearly indicating that she hoped it was untrue, "Were you just putting on a face with Kenny all those years, acting as if you were indifferent to his sexual preference?"

"Oh, gosh, no," Marlene answered. "I'm just excited because now we will get to see him get married and have a family," she worked herself into a kef of delight.

Donna still feared that she had had a candy-coated image of her mom, and it felt like betrayal, so she had little difficulty concealing her relationship with Josh. "Yeah, well, he is confused right now, and I guess I have been focusing more on him than everyone else," Donna lied, saying what she knew her mother wanted to hear.

"Well, we love Kenny very much, you know. Maybe since you guys are getting closer again, you'll bring him over sometime soon?"

"Maybe."

"What about Cam? How's he doing?"

"Good," said Donna, though her mother waited for a more informative answer.

"He's not jealous or anything now, is he?"

Again, Donna gained another layer of understanding and laughed a little as she answered. "No. No, Cam's definitely not jealous of Kenny."

"That's good. What an odd time for all of this to come up— you know, right before your wedding, and all." Marlene failed miserably at trying to sound breezy.

"Look, Mom, Kenny didn't even know I was getting married until after he told me he wasn't gay. He already had a girlfriend before he told me."

"Well, maybe he just played like he didn't know. I mean, Belinda and I hadn't seen each other until just this morning, but our circles do have only one degree of separation between them. It's not implausible that she could have found out, then told Kenny he'd better tell you he wasn't gay before it was too late."

Donna could not believe she had to defend so outlandish a position. "Kenny told me before he told his mom, and like I said, he had a girlfriend."

"I heard that girlfriend was awful to him—almost too awful, you know?"

Donna made an unabashed sound of indignation. "Mom, do you even realize what you are suggesting? The only way your theory that Kenny is in love with me—I can't believe I just said that—could work is if he knew I was getting married before I told him, inveigled Tianna into pretending to be a horrible girlfriend so he could get sympathy from me, and get close to me. Then he would have to reveal his feelings, and hope I shared them enough to break it off with Cam, and marry him instead. Do you realize how insanely contrived that is? You have no idea of the state of our interactions over the previous months. There is no way any of that is even remotely possible!"

"I don't think Kenny's psycho. I just think he might have been seeing Tianna to make you jealous."

"You are 100% ridiculous."

"I'm just saying marriages—not even engagements, but marriages—have broken up for less."

"I'm not indulging this a second longer," Donna groaned. "I gotta go."

"Oh, Donna, quit—"

"Bye, Mom," said Donna, and she hung up without waiting to hear her rebuttal.

Donna did not dare look around. She knew other people in her office must have been staring, but she did not regret her response. She was glad she was nowhere in range of Belinda George, or she would have given her an earful for filling her mother's head with such arrant nonsense. Instead, she was now forced to get Kenny to help her convince their mothers that they were not, in fact, dating.

The matter could not wait for the workday to end; Donna texted Kenny to give him a heads up, and to ask him to call her on his next break.

K- Our mothers are in cahoots, and it's no good. They think your new, hetero identity is all for love of me! Can you believe it? Call me next break—we gotta talk. :-D

The message box on Donna's phone lit up faster than it should have been possible for Kenny to respond.

WTF?!

Donna felt the same way. She was glad when he called not two minutes later.

"How, what, where, why?" Kenny shot at her, without even letting her say hello.

"All I know is 'when.' Apparently, they ran into each other at the mall this morning and hatched some crazy fantasy. You know, you saying you are straight, and me being with you when I was supposed to be dress shopping for my wedding to Cameron—" Donna trailed off.

"This is really the limit," Kenny said, sounding pissed, but not pissy, the distinction clearer to Donna now than ever before. "I can just see my mom trying to figure me out—that's how she screwed me up in the first place!"

It was the first time Donna had ever heard Kenny say what she had hinted at during a recent conversation.

"I can just see them spreading it around. They're probably saying they knew it from the start, and how much it pained them to watch us grow up and figure things out on our own." Kenny was livid.

"My mom even suggested that you knew I was getting married before I told you, which is why you told me you're not gay, so that you still had a chance to win me over before I got married," Donna said sardonically, still enraged for the nerve her mother had shown.

Kenny stuttered for a moment before speaking. "I'm sorry your mom got all tangled up in this. I know it's my mom's doing. She just can't accept the fact that I'm not who she always makes me out to be. This time, it's just sick."

Donna was taken aback by these last words. She knew they had probably just come out badly, but did Kenny think the idea of being with her was sick? "I don't know about 'sick…'"

"Don't start in on yourself again. I didn't mean that dating you is sick; I meant that my mother is sick. Why is she so concerned with my love life, anyway? Now she's convinced herself that it was her idea for me to tell you I am straight." Kenny was restraining himself as much as possible; his worksite was even less private than Donna's was.

"I don't know," Donna sighed heavily. "All I know is that we've got to set them right before this gets so out of hand that people start to believe it."

"It's already that out of hand."

"That's why we have to fix it," Donna mandated, punching her fist into her palm with her phone between her ear and shoulder. "My mom sounded like she was eager for grandkids."

"Here's what we're going to do," Kenny said. "We will deny 'more than friends' stuff with words, but let our tone entail ambiguity. It'll be just like the government and the aliens."

Donna smiled a little as she recalled Kenny's theory that there was no government conspiracy to cover up proof of alien existence; government officials were purposefully ambiguous to incite the idea in paranoids that they were hiding something. Her amusement was only a flash, though, as she considered what he was asking her to do.

"You know I don't do games," she grumbled impatiently.

"You'll have a good excuse to blow off any appointment you have with your mom, avoid all wedding talk, and get together with Josh any time you want," Kenny argued.

Before the conversation was over, Donna agreed to go along with it. After all, Kenny was getting his revenge, and she was getting the time she needed to decide if marrying Cameron was what she wanted to do.

Donna went back to Josh's place again that night. The less she was in her apartment, the further away she could remain from her reality. She filled him in on the scheme Kenny and she were trying to pull off.

"You guys are crafty," Josh smiled, looking as though he would not have had the audacity to attempt it.

"It is a little more than my mom probably deserves, but Kenny's has it coming," Donna defended their behavior.

"Not to be cruel, but do you remember the last time a practical joke was played on you? That was not your favorite day."

"No, it wasn't," Donna said somberly. "I met you, though."

"You did," Josh could not deny.

"Well, maybe I am using it as an excuse to see you without having to explain anything, but when I tried to tell her the truth, she cut me off with this idiocy," Donna said bitterly.

Josh knew arguing the point was not going to help their evening. "Do you want to just go get a pizza and forget about it?"

"No," Donna crabbed. "I can't eat pizza today."

"Why not?"

"Because I'm a hundred and twenty-fat and I can't take it any more!" Donna's fit took Josh by surprise, though her four-year-old voice and actions forced him to smile.

"Do you want to go somewhere we can get salad?" he asked, not knowing what else to say.

"I'll eat something terrible anywhere I go. I can't help it."

Josh began tapping his fingers on the coffee table.

"I'm sorry," Donna cringed a moment later, trying not to cry. "Like you said, I am very self-conscious. I'm not as bad as I used to be, but I have gained eight pounds in the last month."

Donna confessed that it had started with the notorious eggplant and gone downhill from there.

Josh was certain she was exaggerating, but let it go. "What do you want to do then?"

"I wish I liked sushi," Donna said, as though he had not spoken.

Josh was tired of not resolving anything. Donna felt the weight of his impatience, but it only made her fret worse. "I'm not hungry. I should just go home— then you could get whatever you wanted."

"Donna, come on, you just got here. I'm not trying to be mean; I'm just hungry. I'll go anywhere; just tell me what you want."

Suddenly, Donna realized that what she wanted was to be with Cameron.

In her silence, Josh offered, "Or take me to the store, show me what you want, and I'll make it."

"You'll make me anything?" She perked up a little.

"Boxed, canned, frozen—you name it."

It was enough to shake her from her mood. "Let's go out. I know how to behave."

Josh was much happier when they finally settled on a place to go.

Originally, Cameron had planned to stay at his parents' house for only a night or two, but now that his stay was going on night five, he was losing faith in his belief that Donna's outside interest was not a threat. On the third night, he fished his stereo, TV, and DVD player out of the boxes in his parents' garage. He began to wish he had brought more clothes and personal effects with him. He had gone to work Monday and Tuesday feeling confident that Donna would call any time, but by Tuesday evening, he had begun to fall apart, calling himself in for the for the rest of the week.

Cameron's younger brother Sean, who still lived at home while he went to college, had taken pity on him, and spent most of Wednesday with him, but even he could not tolerate Cameron's brooding much longer.

"Cam, if you repeat this song one more time, I'm going to rip out my ear drums!" Sean admonished, though his mood was mostly playful.

The Beatles' "No Reply" had been playing repeatedly for the last two hours. After the fifteenth repetition, Cameron could no longer sing the words without crying, though he kept listening to it.

"This is Donna's favorite Beatles tune. Funny, isn't it? Now it describes my life without her," Cameron pondered morosely.

Sean rolled his eyes. "I like Donna and all, but if it was me, I'd be listening to 'The Rat.'"

Cameron took it as an insult toward Donna, but before he went off on her defense, Sean redirected. "Man, I'm trying to be here for you, but you can't dwell on this stuff all day. Why don't we get out of here tonight?"

"I don't want to go anywhere. I think she'll call tonight. It's close to a week now; I bet she's nearly over her curiosity."

"Cameron, just ball it up and call her."

"I told her I would wait for her. If I call her, she'll think I'm pressuring her."

"Maybe you not calling her is making her think you don't really care if she comes back or not. Besides, why do you want a wife who's already cheating on you before you're even married? Isn't that called foreshadowing or something?" Sean got to his feet and lifted the basketball he had brought in with him with a short dribble.

Cameron sat like a lump, not answering.

"God, I don't want to get involved in all this crap. Come play some one-on-one if you feel like it. In the meantime, I'll be alternately kicking Dad's ass and letting him win." Sean left Cameron to his misery, knowing he was not going to take him up on the offer.

In the kitchen, the boys' mom was preparing a plate of peanut butter and jelly sandwich-halves. "How's he doing in there?"

Sean grabbed a sandwich-half and took a huge, unceremonious bite from it before rolling his eyes and huffing. "You deal with him," he answered, still chewing, and took two more halves before hustling out the back door.

She took the remaining sandwich-halves and a glass of milk in to Cameron a minute later. "Here you go, sweetie."

Cameron gave a meager half-smile and thanked her for the offering. "I don't think I've eaten yet today."

"I was pretty sure you hadn't." She smiled back, lingering as if she hoped to be invited in.

"I'm sorry, Mom, but I'd rather just hang in here by myself for awhile, okay? Just let me know wh—if Donna calls."

"Okay," she said, leaving the room with difficulty, wishing she could make him feel better.

When Kenny was a little boy, he loved to play 'grocery store.' It did not seem to matter if he was clerk or shopper; he loved being either. He had a wide variety of fake foods and a little checkout stand and register that he played at for hours, imaging he was running the conveyor belt, weighing the produce, and even bagging the groceries.

Belinda often watched him with delight, he so into it he did not notice. He would dress up with a hat, a purse, jewelry, and a baby to be the shopper, or an apron and a nametag to be a clerk. Taking in his fondness for dressing up, doing voices, and performing, she had been convinced he was going to be an actor.

Kenny hated children's theatre so much, though, that she let him out of it after only a few weeks. Still, the way he carried on so colorfully compared to his peers, always affected her. When he got too old for 'grocery store,' he moved on to 'big kid' games, but still maintained the same aura. By the time he was in junior high, picking out his own clothes and styling his own hair, something dawned on her that seemed to make sense. 'He must be gay,' she concluded blissfully.

The notion never dampened her feelings for him one bit, and in fact, may have made them stronger. She took great pride in his strength of character and never attempted to influence him to the contrary. She could not believe how she had lucked out—ending up with such a bold and independent child.

7

Donna chose to go out with Kenny that Friday night, instead of Josh. She felt herself pulling away from him, as reluctant as she was to do it. Their relationship had accelerated so easily that there was no place else to take it but to bed, though Donna could not make herself want that. She tried to make herself consider the notion, but though she could imagine herself kissing Josh, even making out with him, as soon as the image headed toward sex, it vanished like a poof from an old-fashioned camera. There was no feeling of lust for him like she had for Cameron.

Donna supposed that was why she was at the movies with Kenny, at the theatre closest to his parents' house, where they went nearly every Friday night without fail.

"Is there anything you want to see?" Donna asked, her tone verging upon a bleat.

Kenny looked around furtively, trying to spot his mom and dad without letting them know he had seen them. "I don't care. You can pick."

Donna felt like she was being used. She had no patience for dramatic games and knew she was in a miserable state if she would go this far to avoid her real life. The worst thing was that she could not threaten him with a chick flick, because she would most likely suffer through it more than he would. "Let's see a horror flick. I need something to lighten my mood."

"Okay, whatever," Kenny said, still not paying nearly as much attention to her as he was to scanning the crowd in the lobby, at the ticket box, and in the mall in front of the theatre.

Donna rolled her eyes. "I'm glad we're having such a nice time on our date," she said, almost shouting, in exaggerated nonchalance.

Kenny got the point. "I'm sorry. I'm just nervous. The whole point of coming here is to make sure we get seen together so my mom can be taught a lesson."

"I know, but do you really think it's necessary? How long do you intend to keep this up?"

Kenny shrugged. He moved a step closer to the ticket window before answering. "I don't know. How long do you intend to keep it up with Josh?"

Donna hated the implication of his question, that the game she was playing with Cameron was no less over the top than the one he was playing with his mom. "If you're not careful, I'm gonna make a huge scene and break up with you—so big your mom and dad can't possibly miss it!" She kept her voice low, but got her point across.

"Okay, I'm sorry." Kenny looked at her sincerely. "A horror movie sounds like a good idea to me, too."

From then on, Kenny lost his distraction. He paid for their tickets at the window and again for their snacks at the counter. Donna was not so forgiving that she insisted on paying her way—he had dragged her there, after all—but she eased up on him.

By the time they were ready to sit, they had to wait another thirty minutes for the previews to begin. Even so, they were lucky to get two seats together that were not in the very front section.

"Good thing we were early," Donna commented as they settled into their seats. "I can't believe how full this place is already."

"I know. I guess Friday night is prime time for movie dates, but I did not imagine this movie would fill up."

"We should have figured, though, since it is date night," Donna said as she took in how many couples surrounded them. "A scary scene is the best excuse for a girl to grab on to her guy." She enacted the suggestion as she spoke it.

"Or for a guy to put his arm around his girl because he thought she was scared," Kenny played along.

They held their pose for a moment, and then broke apart, laughing. "I can't believe this is you and me here acting like this." Donna shook her head, gazing into his eyes for agreement. "Me neither." He looked meaningfully down at her.

A few rows back, Kenny's mom turned to his dad. "Oh, my God!"

Kenny's father responded with minimal interest. "What?"

"I told you. See? I told you!" Belinda beamed as she watched her son playing with his 'old friend.'

"Quit yipping and let them be," Dale George advised her, though he, too, felt a little lighthearted watching them play.

"Maybe he really is straight," Belinda conceded, though the idea still seemed to blow her mind. "Maybe he's had a crush on Donna all along."

"Let's not go jumping the gun. Let them discover it for themselves, like you should have done in the first place."

Dale had not realized he said too much until he felt a quick elbow to his ribs. "Ow!" he cried, stifling it as much as possible.

"What are you trying to say, Dale?" Belinda's teeth were clenched despite her sugary tone.

Dale groaned. "I'm sorry I brought it up. Can we please talk about this when we get home?"

"That's great. You just claimed that I screwed up our son, and you expect me to just sit here, watch a movie, and have a nice time?"

"For one, that's not what I said," Dale started. "For another, if we get up now, they might see us. Let's just leave them alone. I'm sorry if I ruined your night. I didn't mean to, but let's not spoil their evening, too. Imagine how hurt they would be if they thought we were spying on them."

Belinda did not like her position, but she accepted it, crossing her arms and leaning back in her seat, resigned to be there for the duration of the film. To keep her spirits up, she kept imagining the phone call she would make to Marlene DiSimone the next morning. Distant thoughts of grandbabies and holidays with the DiSimones began to form in her mind, though those were yet too far away for even her to consider. Then a crushing thought hit her. If Kenny and Donna really were an item, what had happened to Donna's fiancé? Maybe Marlene had been ready for him to be part of their family; she would think Kenny was a home-wrecker. Then again, Donna did not technically have a home with Cameron yet.

When the lights dimmed, all Dale hoped was that the new couple would not start making out during the previews. That would be too much to handle.

"Marlene, you'll never believe what we saw last night at the movies!" Belinda bubbled with delight as she gossiped to her old friend.

"If it was that good, I guess I want to know."

"What? Oh, no, not the movie—are you kidding? The movie was awful. I'm talking about the *kids*, Marlene!"

"What kids?" asked Marlene, confused.

"*Our* kids—at the movies—together," Belinda explained, straining to keep her tone free of scorn.

Marlene hesitated, afraid to step on Belinda's toes, as she was obviously ardent about the topic.

Belinda continued, "I know it *sounds* normal, but if their body language was any indication, I think our theory from the other day was correct."

"What'd they say when you saw them? Did they look nervous?"

"We were already sitting when they entered the theatre, and they sat a couple rows ahead of us. They had no idea we were there," Belinda said, as though it added credibility to her assumption.

Marlene was coming around too upon hearing that. "You don't say?" She paused as she began to realize what it meant. "You think she's cheating on Cameron? I can't believe she'd do that." Heartbreak was evident in her tone.

Belinda felt a little guilty for enjoying the situation. "I know it's hard to believe, but Donna and Kenny would be so great together! They have loved each other their whole lives, and now they are finding that there is something deeper to explore."

Marlene thought Belinda was beginning to sound like a Lifetime movie. "I guess we'll have to see what unravels. Don't get me wrong—I adore the idea of having Kenny as a son-in-law, but I had taken to Cameron quite well, too."

"Yeah," Belinda said, though she did not sound too affected. "Just picture it, though—you and I, together at Babystyle—Oh, God, Marlene. Halloween outfits!"

Marlene liked the image, but felt that Belinda was going overboard. "Okay, let's not let this get out of hand until we know for sure."

"If you were there last night—"

"But I wasn't, so I need something more solid. I need a straightforward answer," Marlene insisted.

Belinda sounded disappointed, but eventually agreed it could not hurt to have hard evidence. "Why don't you try calling Donna again? I can't call Kenny," she admitted. "Ever since the whole 'straight' thing came up, he's been kind of *off* me, if you know what I mean."

"Hmm," Marlene thought. "What if we all had dinner together?"

"That would never work. From what you said about your last conversation with Donna, she'll know it's a trap if you invite them both some place."

"I guess you're right." Marlene sounded defeated. "We could ambush them—but that wouldn't be very nice."

"We definitely don't want our meddling to put them *off* each other."

Kenny's dad finally decided to pipe up. "Why don't you two just leave the kids alone?"

Belinda ignored him outright.

"Was that Dale?"

"Yes," Belinda affirmed.

"I may have one idea," Marlene said slyly. "I could drop by Donna's apartment with some wedding stuff, then kind of snoop around to see if Cameron's things are still there."

"That's good, but only if Cameron is already on to it, too. If Cameron thinks nothing is up, maybe the place won't look any different."

Dale finally shut off the TV and left the room in a huff. Once he got to his bedroom, he locked the door and picked up his cell phone.

"Hello," said Kenny unsuspectingly.

"Ken, it's Dad," he said in a hushed voice.

"Dad? Why are you whispering?"

"I don't want your mother to hear me. She's on the phone with Marlene DiSimone."

"You don't say?" Kenny asked knowingly.

"She and I saw you with Donna at the movies last night."

"You did?" Kenny fought not to sound too excited.

Dale took his son's excitement to be nerves. "I don't know how much time I have, so I'll tell you that the two of them are cooking up a scheme to get you and Donna to admit you are dating." Kenny tried to interrupt, but Dale held the floor. "I don't care about it one way or the other. I think Donna's a great girl, and it would be wonderful to see you two together, but I'm not as convinced as your mother is that you admitted you were straight just to chase after Donna."

Kenny smiled. Finally, someone seemed to understand him. "You're right, Dad. There's nothing between Donna and me. It's all a hoax to teach Mom to mind her own business and to accept me as I am, not mold me into what she wants me to be."

Dale sighed. "How long are you planning to go on with this? They're already planning your kids' Halloween costumes."

Kenny burst out laughing. "Okay, I guess it's gone far enough," he conceded. "I'll call and tell her it was all for show."

"I don't know how easily she'll be convinced. I think you've dug yourselves into a hole. Plus, I saw you two at the theatre, too, and it really looked like you were flirting."

"I assure you we weren't," Kenny stated. "It was all a show. I was hoping you and Mom would see us together and think we were a couple, but I never saw you, so I figured it hadn't worked."

"What?"

"I know it was dumb, but Mom is just putting so much pressure on me. I guess I took it a little further than I needed to." Kenny bowed his head.

"Kenny, you went to some lengths."

"I know. Donna didn't want any part of it. She just came to do me a favor." Kenny admitted.

"I don't know what to think. How do I know this whole conversation isn't a cover up? Maybe your mother was right."

"Dad, come on. I'm coming clean, okay?"

"So, there's nothing going on between you two?"

"No."

"And, Donna's not cheating on Cameron—everything is still on with their wedding?"

That was where it got tricky for Kenny. He was supposed to be 'coming clean,' but he also felt everyone should mind his or her own business; who was he to tell on Donna? The conversation was specifically about Donna cheating with him, though, so it did give him an out.

"Yeah," he said.

"Well, you had better talk to your mother and get this straightened out; I'm going nuts with all of her yipping and yapping."

Kenny felt bad. Sometimes he wished he could be callous without remorse, as Jay and Greg had been on April Fool's Day. "Okay. Do you want to put her on, or should I call the house?"

"It depends on whether or not she and Marlene are still blithering like idiots."

"That bad, huh?"

"You don't want to know, trust me. Hold on." Dale went to see if Belinda was still on the line.

As he waited for his dad to return, Kenny began to feel ashamed. How old was he?

A few moments later, his mother's voice came on the line. "Kenny?"

"Hi, Mom."

"Dad told me what you guys were talking about," Belinda said cautiously.

"Yeah. I'm sorry it got so out of hand. I had no idea that you and Mrs. DiSimone would get *that* excited about the prospect of Donna and me getting together."

"Well, I am disappointed. Marlene and I were really excited to be related."

"That's part of what got me so mad in the first place, Mom. If it were true that Donna and I were dating, it wouldn't necessarily mean we would get married. You can't be planning my life and telling me how to feel about other people all the time. You have to let me be myself and choose my own significant others."

"Kenny, I'm sorry. I didn't mean to push you in one direction or other," Belinda said sincerely.

"Well, you did. For fifteen years, you convinced me I was gay and only encouraged me down that path. Then, when I discovered I had only been trying to fit into a mold, and it was not who I really am, there you were, already forming another path to push me down. Mom, I'm not gay; you can't parade me around using the gay catch phrases anymore, and I didn't decide this because I had a deep, burning love for Donna. It's me, Mom. Sorry if 'normal' isn't enough for you."

"Kenny, don't give me that crap. I admit I infringed a little, but it was always because you seemed to enjoy it. You constantly reassured me that you were the way I perceived you, so how could I have known that you weren't?"

"You could have looked at me. I feel like the athlete that doesn't even like the sport he plays, but since he's good at it, his parents push him." The drop in Kenny's tone conveyed the weariness he felt.

"I don't know what to say. I guess I was wrong," Belinda admitted simply. "Should I start calling you Ken or talking to you in locker room lingo?"

Kenny laughed. "Mom, I know you'll always support me, but you don't have to go all the way. I'm going to be twenty-five this year; maybe you can treat me like a normal adult," he suggested bravely, though his tone lightened as he continued. "Though, I'll always be your only child at Christmas, or when we go out to dinner—"

Belinda laughed, too. Dale, who had been watching the whole thing, smiled.

Donna was shocked to learn the degree to which her mom and Kenny's mom had invested themselves in their marriage plans. She did not know what disturbed her more—the mental image of being married to Kenny, or that her mom was so willing to write Cameron off as her son-in-law. The former was nothing against Kenny. He was smart, handsome, and caring, but he was like a brother to her. If it had been that hard for her to picture sleeping with Josh, there was no way she could do it with Kenny. Then she realized that she was the one who should be blamed for writing off Cameron, not her mother.

At the end of her evening with Josh on Saturday night, Donna felt incredibly pressured to stay at his house, in his bed this time. She had done all she could to keep at least a foot away from him at all times, but she was close to slipping, and Josh could sense it.

"Donna, I'm trying to respect your wishes, but it really hurts me every time you turn away from my kiss or recoil from my touch. I can't help taking it personally," Josh finally confessed when Donna shot up from her seat on the couch the moment Josh sat next to her.

"I'm sorry," Donna sniffed. She wanted to comfort him, but knew what it would lead to.

"I miss being close to you—being able to hug you. You're making me feel like I should be ashamed of myself—like I am dirty or something."

"It's not like that," Donna said, though her statement was not entirely accurate. One of Donna's biggest hang-ups was that he had been with many other women, and though most of them were years in the past, it still bothered her. "I don't understand it myself. I know it sounds lame, or sheltered or childish, but I just can't see us actually—"

"Don't try to analyze it; just feel it. Sometimes you have to trust your senses."

Donna looked at him incredulously.

"I'm not trying to use a line on you," Josh groaned. "I've never shown you anything but respect. I am this close to loving you," he measured a distance between his thumb and forefinger, "but I can't get past the way you make me feel when you shudder at just the suggestion of intimacy."

At that moment, Donna realized something. Josh was a *real* person. Had she been toying with him all this time? Here he was, almost in love with her, and all she could think about was finding a polite way to get out of there without having to sleep with him.

Her conclusion must have been evident in her features; Josh's face fell. "I don't like that look," he whimpered.

"I'm really sorry," Donna said, starting to cry. "I wasn't trying to play with your emotions. I didn't understand what I was doing."

"I don't think you have been." He made a plea.

"I have, though. I just realized. I was never fully invested in this relationship. I saw it as a phase or trial; I never fully dissociated myself from Cameron. I still want to marry him."

Josh was taken aback. He thought all her plans of getting back together with Cameron had been deserted. "I can't believe I was dumb enough to think you chose me." He took off his glasses, rubbing his eyes.

The feeling of breaking up was becoming familiar to Donna, and she hated it.

"I feel like a skipping disc, but all I can say is, 'I'm sorry.' I know it's not worth much, but it was not intentional. This is so weird. Most people experience what I am feeling much earlier in life, but where other people my age are practiced; I'm still practicing." She shrugged, looking at him with honesty, crying very little. "I don't suppose you'll forgive me. Hell, I don't even know if Cameron will forgive me, but it's worth it to try to get him back."

Josh's posture sunk lower.

"He was very confident I would come back, though, so hopefully he still wants me to," Donna finished, feeling guilty.

Josh was glad she was done talking about Cameron. "So, you're gonna go back to him, then?" he asked, though it was more of a statement than a question.

Donna nodded. "Yeah. I think I'm ready."

"Good for you, then." Josh was depressed, but not derisive. "Cameron goes back to being the lucky guy, and I go back to being whatever I am. It must be my comeuppance for not falling for you in high school when I had a chance."

"It wouldn't have worked back then, either. If you think I am a basket case now, be glad you didn't know me then." They both laughed a little. "We both have done a lot since then to improve ourselves. I lost weight, which had always been heavier on my mind than my body, and you went to Hong Kong, improved your tenor, and rediscovered your love of writing. None of that would have happened if we had gotten together in high school."

The truth did little to improve his emptiness. "Good luck with Cameron, I guess," Josh sighed, stretching his arms across the back of the couch.

After an awkward moment, he broke the silence by saying, "Well, I'm gonna have a beer. You want one last perfect gin and tonic?"

"I'd love one, but I probably shouldn't just pound it right before I hit the road, and I don't think I could stay more than a few minutes." Donna sounded regretful.

"Yeah. I suppose we shouldn't prolong the inevitable."

Donna nodded. "I guess I'll be going, then."

"I guess so," Josh agreed, standing and approaching her.

For the first time, Donna did not need to pull away. She no longer distrusted herself. They shared a meaningful embrace and separated without words. She left Josh wearing the most vanquished expression she had ever seen.

Donna went home, full of thoughts of Cameron, but she did not call him. Her realization was too newly formed. Even though she had broken it off with Josh, she was not quite ready to take the next step.

Monday morning, Cameron's mother had to force him out of bed when Donna still had not called. He left for work on autopilot, numb, barely participating in the world.

Later that morning, Tony Loria had to do some pushing, too. He had had enough with his sister Tianna's refusal to face facts and be a responsible human being.

"Look, Tia, no one's asking you to marry the guy." He shook a finger at her.

"But, he's a f—" With one look from Tony, she stopped before she finished the word. "He's a you-know-what. What's he gonna do with a baby? If I do what I want to do, then neither of us will have to suffer."

"He wasn't a you-know-what the day he impregnated you," Tony refuted. "You never even gave him a chance to explain that letter, either. Maybe it wasn't what you thought."

"It was a love letter to someone named Marcos. Have you ever heard of a girl named Marcos?"

"Either way, you owe him at least the knowledge. If you want, I'll place the call, but you have to promise to be civil when he gets here."

Tianna pouted, crossing her arms in front of herself, but not arguing.

Tony walked over to the phone mounted on the wall near the swinging doors that led from the kitchen to the dining room. "What's the phone number?"

"I don't remember," she said obstinately.

"Tia, I swear to God, if you don't stop acting like a—"

"555-8616," she said loudly.

"Was that so goddamn difficult?" he sneered, waiting for the first ring to sound.

Kenny's voice mail eventually answered. Tony waited for the prompt, and then said, "Kenny, this is Tony Loria. I know you and Tianna aren't exactly getting along these days, but will you please call me back at the restaurant? 555-0104. Looking forward to hearing from you, buddy." He hung the receiver back on the wall.

Tianna groaned. She had hoped to finish this. "If he doesn't call back tonight, I'm doing what I have to do," she snapped. "There's only so much of a window to perform the procedure."

"Shut up, Tianna! You are not having an abortion unless Kenny agrees that you should. And you have to wait at least another few days after that to be sure."

"Shut up or Dad might hear," she squeaked.

"Yeah, you're lucky he doesn't know. He would be trying to get you and Kenny married, though he might feel too sorry for Kenny to go through with it."

"You're funny," she laughed sarcastically. "It doesn't matter, anyway. I'm not going to have this baby, and Dad never needs to know I was pregnant."

Tony had never wanted to slap some sense into her more than he did just then. "Tia, this is a baby. Even if you don't have the decency to raise it yourself—thank God for being gracious enough not to let you want to raise a baby—someone out there wants to. So, even though Kenny does not strike me as one to abandon his parental duties, if you both decide not to keep it, you should at least put it up for adoption."

"Fat chance! I'm not going through all that pain and sickness and wrecking my body for someone else to have a baby."

"Get out of my kitchen!" he yelled at her, unable to take it any longer.

For the first time, Tianna looked frightened. "Tony—" she started, but he wasn't kidding.

"Stay out of my face until I come to tell you what time you're meeting Kenny," he snarled.

Tianna did not try to come back. She eased herself out from under him and scampered through the swinging doors. Tony fumed afterward, trying to figure out how he was going to run a restaurant and get through the day without throttling his sister.

"I'll just keep reminding myself she's pregnant," he said under his breath, sighing and trying to get a grip on his emotions.

Kenny called Tony back a couple of hours after he had left the message, intrigued as to why he was calling. Even after their brief conversation, he was still unclear as to why he had agreed to come down to the restaurant when he got off work that afternoon.

He drove up to the front doors of Loria, feeling similar to the way he felt when pulling up to Marcos' apartment complex. As he approached the restaurant door, he saw Tianna's father, Stefano, shoot him a furtive look.

Stefano's eyes moved immediately back to whomever he was entertaining, but he knew something strange was going on; Kenny was coming back around, and Tony and Tianna had been avoiding each other and not speaking all day.

Tony also saw Kenny as he entered. He hurried up to him, greeted him fondly, and then quickly ushered him to the back office, as though he did not want Kenny to be seen. He even checked that the coast was clear before closing the door and locking it.

"Okay, this is getting weird," Kenny said openly.

Tony's eyes said, 'You don't know the half of it,' as he took a moment to collect himself.

"Does Tianna know I'm here?"

"Yeah, she does," Tony answered.

"Then what's all the secrecy about?"

Tony pulled out a chair and pushed Kenny into it, still looking over his shoulder every other second. "Actually, it's Dad. He sees you as the guy who broke his little girl's heart, though I know better."

Kenny almost started on a defensive rant about whose heart had been broken the day Tianna found the letter, but he could tell by looking at Tony that it was unnecessary and not nearly as important as the reason Kenny had been asked there in the first place. "Yeah, he looked at me kinda funny as I was walking in."

"Crap!" Tony exclaimed, slamming his fist on the desk he leaning against. "I should have had you come in the back way."

"He hates me that much?" Kenny sounded hurt.

"No, no. Just sit tight while I get Tianna." Kenny looked nervous. "Don't worry, this is not a ploy to get you back together; I don't wish that on you." He gave a hint of a genuine smile.

Kenny did not respond. He just waited for Tony, who had zoomed out of the room, to return, though he did not necessarily want Tianna to come back with him.

The two did eventually return, and Kenny saw Tony's arm as he urged Tianna into the office and heard his muffled voice as he whispered to someone in the hall to keep their dad busy. Once again, the door was locked before anything was said.

Tianna scowled haughtily at Kenny as she took the seat opposite him.

"All right, Tia. We're in the back room to protect your privacy, so don't go flying off the handle and drawing anyone in here," Tony warned sternly.

"I'm sorry, what private matter are we protecting here?" Kenny asked.

"You know how this starts," Tony prodded Tianna.

After a lengthy, frustrated sigh, she spoke stiffly. "I'm sorry for calling you a faggot."

"You don't sound very sorry," Tony observed, not looking at Kenny.

Tianna cleared her throat. "I'm sorry I called you that. I jumped to a conclusion, and it was wrong of me to be so mean, whether or not you did write a love letter to a dead guy."

Tony was losing his patience, but he looked to Kenny as though it was his turn to speak.

"Am I supposed to defend myself or something? Why are we here?"

120

"You don't have to answer to anyone. Just tell Tianna if you accept her apology."

"I guess so."

"Good. Now that we are remaining civil to each other," Tony mediated, "Tianna, what do you have to tell Kenny?"

Tianna held her lips tightly together as though trying to prevent the words from bursting out of her. It only lasted for a few seconds before she let go. "I'm pregnant."

Kenny's eyebrows threatened to jump over his forehead. "What?" he spat.

Tony might have been watching a ping pong match at the rate his eyes flicked from one to the other, then back again.

"Yes," she exaggerated. "Just give me your okay, and I'll get rid of it."

Kenny was confused. "Get rid of it?"

"You know, have an a—"

"Don't say the A-word!" Tony cringed as he turned to watch the door, afraid their dad would break through it at any moment. "An unmarried Catholic woman does not use the A-word in this building, got it?"

"I think you know what I mean," Tianna finished.

"You want my okay?" Emotion was building in Kenny so rapidly he did not know how long he could keep his voice down.

"You want a baby?" she mimicked.

"Yes!" Kenny said, not knowing it was going to come out. Even he had to take a moment to consider what he had said, though gratification was already showing on Tony's face.

Tianna remained dubious. "What are you and your boyfriend gonna do with a baby? The court probably wouldn't even let you keep it. Then I'd be stuck with it."

"I don't have a boyfriend; I'm not gay. That poem was written for my very best friend in college. I can't explain our relationship in a nutshell, but I assure you that I have no inclinations toward men."

Tianna looked like she was beginning to believe him. "Even if you're not, how do you expect to take care of a baby all by yourself? Believe me, I want no hand in it."

Kenny shrugged. "I don't know, I guess I'll find a way to manage, right? That's what millions of other people do." A huge grin was spreading across his features as he began to take in what he was saying. A glee completely new to him raced through his body.

"I can't believe this," Tianna said, fed up, looking to Tony for support.

But Tony's purpose had been fulfilled. "I knew it! I knew you would never agree to an abortion!"

"Abortion!" roared Stefano Loria as he erupted through the door.

"So much for protecting my privacy," Tianna sneered at her brother.

"Tia, you are with child?"

She hung her head and nodded.

"And, this faccio is the father?"

"He's not really a-a- one of those," Tianna explained as politely as she knew how.

Kenny felt a tiny bit vindicated.

Stefano looked angrier that he had not been informed than befuddled by the news. "Tianna, you are unmarried. You must now get married to redeem yourself."

'To each other?' Kenny wanted to ask, but held it in.

"Dad, there's not going to be any wedding," Tony started firmly.

"Well, there can be no abortion," his father replied, then turned to Tianna. "We will send you to a convent where you can live until you can leave the baby."

"Dad, she's not fifteen, and these are modern times. She's a grown woman." Tony paused. "By the way, where the hell is Vinny? He was supposed to be watching the door."

"I gave him the slip," Stefano answered dismissively.

"I'll take care of it," Kenny piped up. "I won't ask for child support, if you don't want to give it, and I will even pretend I don't know you, if that's what you prefer."

"Yes." Tianna jumped on the offer.

"No!" Stefano roared again. "It's my grandchild, I will pay."

"Everyone, just hold on here. This is a bad time to make promises. Tianna, the closer you come to having this baby, you might change your mind."

"So, what are my rights to see you during the pregnancy?" Kenny asked, surreptitiously taking Tianna's hands and looking into her eyes as though they were the only two in the room.

Normally, Tianna would have had some cheeky reply, but even she could not find something nasty to say. "You mean it?"

"Yeah. All of a sudden, I don't hate you, anymore." He smiled stupidly.

She returned the smile, gazing at him differently, too.

Tony and his dad looked at each other incredulously.

"I guess you could come by after work sometimes, or maybe Saturdays? Probably not until I get bigger, though—"

"You can page my phone any time you need me. I don't care if you're depressed, hungry, hairy, or what. I'll be there," Kenny pledged.

Tianna was taken aback by his kindness.

"You are the mother of my child," he shrugged and smiled again. "No matter what happens."

The other two men could not help but smile, too. "I am a grandfather!" Stefano proclaimed.

"I'm an uncle!" Tony shouted, and they each hugged Tianna and Kenny in turn.

Kenny stayed at the restaurant for hours, opening bottles of wine and eating. By the end of the night, he was elated. He could not imagine ever feeling a greater high.

When she was in eighth grade, Donna's family got what, at the time, was an extremely compact and advanced video camera. Before its days of recording MistaSista, Kenny and Donna spent a lot of time writing scripts and making sets for movies with Barbie adults and G.I. Joe babies. The plots usually entailed elements of horror and sci-fi, and cardboard box dioramas were fashioned into sets, often with Construx and Lego furniture and props. The actors were made into marionettes and were walked around by hopping on two feet. Any time an actor's position had to change, the tape would pause, and the figure would jerk to the new position when filming resumed.

Despite the crudeness of their efforts, they were very proud of their work and displayed the choppy productions to anyone they could sucker into watching them.

One day, they were designing a set, and Donna, who was more resourceful, though far from meticulous, was describing her vision of how it should look.

"Well, it's supposed to be a single dad with a son, so I don't think it should be so clean," she commented. "We should put some clothes on the floor or dishes on the table—"

Kenny had been picturing a nuclear family. "I thought there was going to be a mom."

"No, this one is supposed to be like you when you're grown up," she stated, not intending anything negative. "Mine will have a mom and a dad."

Kenny felt sad, though he tried not to show it.

Seeing his disappointment, Donna added, "Well, maybe yours could have two dads, then the other dad can be the clean one." She shrugged, willing to go along with it if it would appease him.

8

D onna was getting ready to leave work when Kenny called her, sounding almost mischievous.

"Is something going on?" she finally asked, feeling he had been beating around the bush.

"Yes!" he beamed—glad she had finally asked.

"Well, what?"

"Okay, let me first say that I do wish I didn't have to tell you this on phone, but I am on my way to do something, so I can't go all the way out there right now." He paused, sighing audibly. "I am on my way to pick up Tianna."

"What?"

"I know, it's totally crazy, but I'm taking her to meet my parents tonight."

"Kenny, I thought you were done screwing with them about your sex life." Donna sounded disappointed.

"I am."

"No way! You guys are not back together—tell me you're not!"

Kenny made a noncommittal sound. "'Together's a strong word right now, but we will never be completely out of each others' lives again."

Donna was stunned. "You're not saying that she's—" Donna could not even say it aloud.

"I'm gonna be a dad!"

Donna thought she might drop the phone onto her desk and pass out.

"Look, I'm sure this sounds nuts. That's how I first felt, but after discussing it for a bit— I don't know—there's just something different about Tianna now."

"Did she get a common courtesy implant or something?"

"Not precisely, but I think she's getting there," Kenny answered thoughtfully.

"I can't believe this. Don't you remember what a horrible bitch she was?"

"Very much so," Kenny admitted flatly. "But as soon as I told her I would rather take the baby on my own than her have an abortion, something changed."

"You had an out?" Donna was flabbergasted.

"I never saw it that way. I mean, maybe if I was sixteen—but at twenty-four, I don't really see that as an option any more. Besides, I'm ecstatic!"

"You're insane," Donna corrected. "There is going to be so much drama..." She shook her head unable to fathom what was to come. Trying to look on the bright side, though, she added, "but on the other hand, eggplant is back on the menu!"

"There might be a ton of drama," Kenny agreed, "but just knowing I have a little baby growing inside of her—" He trailed off, overcome with giddiness.

"I thought things were finally getting back to normal."

"Actually, it's good. Tony and Stefano are both incredibly supportive—it was actually Tony that got her to tell me about it."

Donna groaned with disbelief.

"Besides, how can things be back to normal if you are still on the fence about Cameron?" Kenny led.

"I broke it off with Josh on Saturday night," Donna confessed, defeated. "I still don't know what the hell I was doing with him."

"Me, neither, but *Saturday*? And you still haven't told me?"

"Sorry. I haven't gotten the nerve up to talk to Cameron yet, and I guess I didn't want to say anything until I knew where we stood."

"Well, just go tell him you want him back."

Donna made an indignant sound.

"I'm serious. Tianna almost made the worst mistake by acting without telling me what was going on. The second I knew about it—it was like it was no big deal any more."

"Are you guys getting married?" Donna asked, closing her eyes and bracing herself.

"Are you and Cameron?" He waited. "You still want to."

"You're right." Donna's voice gained some strength. "I'm just gonna go over to his parents' house and tell him. If he's already over me, then I fucked up, and I have to get on with my life—all this overanalyzing is making me crazy."

"Good girl," Kenny congratulated. "Things will be normal again soon—I'm gonna be a dad, and that's more normal than anything I've ever been!"

Donna could not believe his enthusiasm. She had never seen anything like it. It inspired her to become as happy as he seemed to be.

It was about six o'clock in the evening when Donna finally approached Cameron's house. She parked along the sidewalk, seeing it differently than she had in the past. His parents had obviously done well for themselves and their children, but their house still had a humble element to it, despite the perfectly manicured lawn, the finely masoned façade, and the luxury cars parked in the garage. She wanted to bring her children here for Christmas. Cameron ought not to be in residence here without her.

As shaky as she felt, it was hard enough for Donna to make her way up the driveway without the basketball flying at her head. She threw her arms up to protect her face, and the ball bounced harmlessly off them. After she screamed, she heard voices from behind the side gate and the sounds of someone running toward her.

"Sorry about that, Donna." Sean apologized sheepishly as he met up with her on the driveway and collected the ball.

"It's okay," she replied. "It didn't get me too hard."

"That was the first one that's gone over the wall in ages." Sean sounded more amazed than concerned.

"Hopefully, Cameron didn't throw it at me on purpose, though I don't think I could blame him."

"Are you kidding?" Sean asked. "I have been trying to get his ass out of his room for days, but all he will do is mope."

Donna could not help but be a little flattered, in spite of the guilt she felt for putting him through this.

"I swear, if I hear 'No Reply' one more time—" Sean's irritation built faster than he could think. "But you're here, so does that mean?"

Donna's smile was all nerves.

Sean smiled back, then cheered. "Yes! You gotta take him back; I've had enough."

Talking to Sean made Donna feel more comfortable about being there. He also made it sound like Cameron had been miserable without her, and was therefore likely to grant forgiveness.

"Tell you what—you come inside and wait downstairs, and I'll make sure he pulls himself together enough to avoid making a complete ass out of himself." Sean motioned for her to follow as he headed back through the gate.

They passed the boys' father as they went through the backyard and into the kitchen. Mr. Ellis just grinned as he watched her enter the house. Donna had a grim flash of what his reaction might have been had she had called here that fateful night and asked for an update of the proceedings for his eldest son's funeral.

As Sean piloted Donna into the kitchen, his mother's jaw dropped, and she jumped to her feet in surprise. "Mom, don't do anything crazy," Sean warned, gesturing to her to stay put, as though she might attack Donna with kisses.

"No, no," she almost cried. "I'm just so glad you're here, sweetie!" She put a hand over heart as she continued to take in Donna's presence, still not entirely sure that she was there.

Sean rolled his eyes. "Whatever," he said. "I'm going up to get Cameron. Just keep calm, and Donna—don't you dare run out."

After getting non-verbal commitments from each woman, he took off up the stairs and pounded on Cameron's door.

"Cam!" he yelled. "Get your clothes on and get your butt downstairs."

"Go away!" Cameron roared back, wishing Sean would let him wallow.

"Trust me, you want to come down." He lowered his voice a little.

There was a scrambling from the room and Cameron's voice sounded as though it was an inch from the other side of the door. "Is Donna on the phone?"

"No." Sean heard Cameron's hope dying and saved it. "She's in the kitchen."

Sean backed away as the door was flung open. He grinned when he saw Cameron's desperate, 'Don't mess with me' expression. "Put some pants on, and pretend like you've showered since Thursday."

Cameron gazed at him sternly, trying to discern any hint of a practical joke. When he was at last willing to believe his little brother, he said. "I showered yesterday morning—Mom made me."

His smile was ear-to-ear as he galloped down the stairs a moment later, straightening immediately as he hit the bottom floor and turned for the kitchen. He was as cool as he could manage upon setting eyes on Donna. Donna looked up from her half-begun cup of coffee and almost cried; it felt longer than a week and a half since they had parted ways. Cameron's mother silently backed out of the room, jabbing Sean in the ribs to get him to do the same.

It was a little eerie for Donna, knowing that Cameron's whole family was watching them from outside, but she forgot all about it when Cameron began to speak.

"Hi," he started in a brittle voice.

"Hi," Donna eked out before she began crying.

Cameron put his arms around her, and it felt natural, unlike the last several days without her had felt. Donna felt the healing effect of the embrace, and reveled in it, like a mewling kitten.

"Does this mean you forgive me?" Cameron asked after a moment of silent rocking.

Donna sprung out to face him. "Forgive you?" she asked incredulously. "I'm the one stupid enough to let a little attention almost ruin our lives."

Cameron laughed, now secure in that whatever had happened between Donna and Josh was in the past. "Well, you came back, so you must have found your common sense at some point."

"Yeah. I realized it right before it was too late." She felt the hint of celebration that coursed through Cameron's body. "You can relax. I hardly even let him kiss me on the cheek. I just couldn't—and I didn't want to."

"I really don't want to talk about it any more than necessary, but can you promise me that you will never be swept up by your curiosity again?" Cameron asked.

"Never." Donna stressed the word as hard as she could. "We got along awesomely as friends, but as soon as anything further was invoked, everything enticing about him just shut off. There was nothing of the lust I feel for you." She stared earnestly into his eyes. "I had just never had that kind of attention before, and I didn't know how to handle it. I know most guys would not believe me, and certainly not forgive me, but—"

"I'm not most guys. I love you, and I have waited for you to come back."

"I'm glad, though I gather it's been a pretty rough week," Donna said awkwardly.

"Ten days," Cameron corrected, mostly in jest.

"Well, obviously my relationship with Josh could not compare to the one I have with you; ours lasted fewer days than yours and mine was suspended. It must have just been a little 'Moonlight Madness.'"

Cameron looked confused.

" Well, I know that most Golden Girls references would be lost on you—which I still don't get because you love Will & Grace, which is essentially the same show in a different setting," Donna vented, "but this one goes all the way back to Shakespeare. It's just the idea that all this craziness could go on in one night, but it's almost like a dream by the time you wake up."

"A Midsummer's Night Dream?" Cameron asked, beginning to understand.

Nodding, Donna stated, "Yeah, only I needed more than just one night to be sure that's all it was." She drew back the corner of her mouth in shame, not meeting his eyes.

Cameron smiled, and gathered her back into his arms.

More confident, in the safest place on Earth, she went on, "I must have been confused by the whole April Fool's thing. It really messed with my mind, even more than I knew until just these last couple of days. I think my leaving you had to do with the fear of you leaving me. I can't believe it was strong enough to take over. I had thought nothing could."

"It didn't really take over," he assured her, still hugging her tight. "Like you said, our relationship was merely suspended; it wasn't even as much as a hiatus."

Donna felt his hands leave her back as he gestured, then land gently back upon her. She let the feeling take prominence over a similar memory involving Josh. Over her head, Cameron could see his family pretending they were not spying. "We better let everyone else back in, so they can have audio," he laughed, urging her to turn so she, too, could catch them in the act.

"That's it?" Donna asked—her eyes innocent. "You're not going to yell at me? You don't want time to consider—"

"No. I told you how I feel about you. I don't need to play games to maintain a macho image. I don't want to hurt your feelings to give you a taste of your own medicine. It's pointless. I only care that I have you."

"I just can't believe it's so easy." Donna was relieved.

"It always will be with us. I just want to get on with planning our wedding, and hope nothing else ever gives us such a trial."

Donna smiled, on the verge of tears. "I have one last thing to ask before you let them in."

Cameron remained serious.

"'Poodles and lampshades?'" she asked, indicating that it was the oddest description she had ever heard.

Cameron shrugged diffidently, looking adorably blameless. "It was one of those 'heat of the moment' phrases."

Outside, Cameron's mother cooed to his father. "Aw, they're laughing."

Donna could hardly believe she had glided through the whole process, as Cameron's family rejoined them a moment later.

"Thank God you came back before we had to throw him out." Sean patted her on the back blithely as he approached the kitchen island, against which she was leaning.

Donna felt shy for the few first few minutes, but once the news of Kenny and Tianna's unborn child was out, she felt more in her element with each zany detail she divulged.

The drive with Tianna to his parents' house went more smoothly than Kenny could have hoped. She had a happy nervousness about her that he had only seen rare glimmers of in the past. It calmed him, a fact he welcomed eagerly, as he knew that the rest of the evening was not likely to be so agreeable. When he parked the car in the driveway, he did not immediately go to open his door, nor did Tianna hers.

They shared an anxious laugh.

"I guess this can't be easy for you, either," Kenny sympathized.

Tianna did not have to speak. Her big, frightened eyes and the way she bit her lip were enough.

Kenny blew out a long sigh. "I wish I could be more comforting, but I'm sure there's going to be awkwardness, and I'm sure my mother is going to say something terribly uncomfortable at every interval she is allowed a word in."

Tianna laughed again, looking as if she would rather stay in the driveway all night than face the Georges.

Finally, Kenny decided that he should take some initiative. He let himself out, then walked around, and opened Tianna's door for her. As they walked up to the house, he wondered if he should have been a little more informative in the call he made to his mother earlier that day. All he had told her was that he had rekindled his relationship with Tianna, and he wanted to begin on an open and honest note. As he had never delved deeply into why they had broken up originally, it was easy to keep the past negativity in the closet.

Kenny was glad his dad answered the door. It was easier to start with a kind face than an eagerly perceptive one.

"Hi, Ken. Your mother is still getting everything in order in the kitchen." Dale smiled warmly as he showed them in.

Kenny noticed that he had been addressed as 'Ken,' but as his dad sometimes called him that, he decided not to get too hung up on whether he was trying to make him sound more masculine in front of Tianna.

"Dad, this is Tianna Loria."

"Naturally." Dale amped up the charm in his voice then took her hand by the fingertips as she went the little step up and over the threshold.

Kenny had his hand gently against the small of her back as she stepped up, and entered closely behind her.

They walked toward the brightly lit kitchen, and Kenny's mom came out to meet them wearing an apron and oven mitts, looking like a picture-perfect homemaker, like someone Kenny had never seen before.

"Tianna!" she said, as though she had been anticipating meeting her for her entire life. "Let's have a look at you! Oh, you are beautiful, just like Kenny said!"

Kenny's first thought was that he had not said, though since Tianna was indeed beautiful, he let it slide. He was thankful that Tianna's heritage allowed her to accept flamboyant greetings from strangers without shrinking away in fright. "You don't have to maul her," he finally said, when Belinda was still smothering his guest a moment later.

Belinda laughed it off gaily. "Well, I am Belinda, and this is Dale, and we'd like to welcome you to our home." She elbowed Dale in the side as a cue to look more gracious.

"Thank you," Tianna said simply, now even less certain she needed to meet Kenny's family.

As they headed into the kitchen, Belinda said, "I hope you find the food to your liking. We'll start with an appetizer salad, move into dinner, and then dessert. I know you are used to restaurant dining and all—"

"I'm sure it will be lovely," Tianna complimented genially.

Kenny lagged behind far enough to share a moment of incredulity with his father.

A few minutes later, Belinda batted her eyelashes as she waited for Tianna's reaction to the salad. At first, Tianna gave her a seemingly rehearsed, positive, intrigued indication, but once the taste had had time to settle, her eyes grew very wide, almost horrified, and she dropped her fork onto her plate with a loud clank and ran for the hall bathroom. Within seconds, retching sounds could be heard from the direction in which she had run. Kenny put down his fork and ran after her.

Dale halted the bite that had been headed for his mouth, sniffing it cautiously. Belinda smacked him with her cloth napkin, looking aghast.

Another long moment later, the sound of a flushing toilet could be heard, and Kenny returned to the table alone. "Ginger," he said awkwardly. "Apparently, she's very intolerant of ginger."

Belinda sounded betrayed. "I told you I was making an Asian appetizer salad! What did you think I would use for dressing—ranch?"

Kenny put up his hands in defense. "I didn't know, honestly. She's not allergic, or anything, she just hates it. She'll be out in a moment as soon as she washes up."

Kenny's mom was still scandalized. "Don't you think that's a little impertinent? I hope you have better manners if you are served something you don't like in a strange house."

Kenny wanted to tell her why Tianna's reaction had been so severe, but did not think the time was quite right.

"How about we just pretend nothing happened?" Dale suggested with a look at his wife as they heard Tianna entering the hall.

"All better?" Kenny asked delicately as she headed back to her seat.

Tianna gave a tiny little nod. "I'm dreadfully sorry, Mrs.—"

"'Belinda,' please, and it's quite all right. I didn't know about the ginger, but the salmon is ginger-free. I hope teriyaki is more to your taste."

Tianna nodded again, but prayed with all her might that she would be able to stomach every other item on the menu.

"Sweetie, there's plenty more salad without dressing on it, and we have several other dressings in the fridge, if you'd like something else," Dale offered kindly.

"Thanks."

"Dad, why don't I?" Kenny said, getting to his feet before Dale had scooted his chair out.

After a few minutes, Tianna began working on a new salad. "I love the oranges and the crunchy noodles," she said after a bit, trying to redeem herself a little, praying that the Georges' future grandchild would cooperate for the rest of the night. And indeed, when Belinda served her fried couscous, even she could not maintain a grudge when Tianna eagerly helped herself to a third generous portion.

"Well, I'm glad someone brought her appetite," she said at last, looking positively delighted, as though the entire evening had been won with one side dish.

"It really is good, Mom," Kenny added, making her cheeks even rosier.

When everyone seemed about finished, including Tianna, who still had time to squeeze in another scoop of couscous and several more spears of broccoli, a growing expectation for conversation began to encroach upon the table. Kenny found himself unprepared to make his announcement, and looking toward Tianna for support was getting him nowhere, as she was concentrating on the floor.

"Well," Kenny clapped his hands together, uncomfortably aware of his parents' eyes upon him, "that was the best I've eaten since my last meal at Loria."

"I read a write-up on it from a local paper, once I knew it was your family's place." Belinda beamed at Tianna. "They had only divine things to say about it. I was telling Dale we must head out there some time—admire the art, sample the cuisine…"

Tianna nodded passively again.

Kenny had never seen her so timid before, and was offput by it. She had always taken charge and made demands; now that he was forced to do it, he missed her overbearing attitude.

"Why don't I clear the plates, since your mother put so much effort into the meal?" Dale offered to soften the silence.

"I could do it," Kenny said, trying to steal the occupation.

"Nonsense," said Belinda. "Why don't you tell us what brought you two back together after all those weeks apart?"

Kenny hesitated. "Well, it's a funny thing. I got a message from Tianna's brother Tony one day," he began nervously.

Tianna looked at him, dread in her features.

"Don't tell me he's the one that got you back together," said Belinda in exaggerated disbelief.

"Sort of." Kenny was choking.

"Tony's always liked Kenny very much." Tianna finally piped up.

"Really?" Belinda appeared to be fighting very hard not to say what she was thinking.

Kenny swore to himself that if she took that moment to make an off-color gay comment, her grandma rights would be severely limited.

Instead, Tianna was allowed to continue, her voice smoother with each syllable. "Yes. Tony knew I needed to talk to Kenny again, and forced me to give him Kenny's number, so he could arrange a meeting between us."

Kenny liked coasting along with whatever she said, though he worried that her story could only stay ambiguous for so long. Eventually, they were going to have to make the announcement.

"Well, it appears that that was a lucky thing, doesn't it?" Belinda goaded her.

Tianna nodded; some of her initial anxiety had apparently worn off. She looked at Kenny, clearly expecting him to comment.

"Yeah, I was pretty surprised, but most surprising was—" even Kenny was not sure what he was going to say, but then Dale dropped a piece of silverware, which clattered loudly in the sink's metal basin.

"Dale!" Belinda chastised, as though he had done it on purpose.

He apologized. "Nothing's broken."

"Never mind. Why don't you just get out the stuff for the chocolate martinis?"

Tianna shot Kenny an exasperated look.

"Uh, Mom, maybe we better skip the liquor tonight."

Belinda looked confused. "I thought you loved martinis?"

"I do. I do." Kenny assured her. "It's just that Tianna can't really drink."

A look as though she had created the grandest faux pas crossed Belinda's face. "Oh, God. I never thought to ask. She is twenty-one, isn't she?"

Tianna spat the water she had just taken back into her glass.

"Mom!" Kenny shrieked. "Of course, she is."

Belinda shrugged unrepentantly.

"It's okay, honey. They can enjoy the cake without the drink." Dale stepped in.

Belinda knew they could, but there were now two strikes against her meal. She was beginning to wonder how many more of Tianna's aversions she would have to compete with for their next dinner over.

"I'm not too young. I am pregnant," Tianna finally admitted.

Even Dale spun around in shock at that. Belinda gaped inelegantly, all happy-hostess endeavors vacated.

"Well, there you have it," Kenny stated.

Dale's stunned gawp morphed into a joyous grin almost as soon as it formed. "Kenny, you're going to be a dad?"

Kenny nodded, going slightly pink.

Dale, who had already abandoned his cocktail supplies, dashed over to hug his son. Though Belinda had been closer to the kids, she had reached for neither. She was still trying to take it in; she had not quite let go of the whole Kenny and Donna fantasy yet.

When Kenny broke out of his dad's embrace, and Dale was on his way to go hug Tianna, he noticed his mom's white face. "Mom, our reunion will not be rushed. We are not planning to be married; we are not planning to even live together right now."

Belinda appeared even further affected by this news. "Kenny, I don't know what to say. I mean, I'm glad you're not just getting married for the sake of the baby, but honey, this is so unexpected."

"That's how I felt at first, too," Tianna dumbed down her actual initial outlook. "Now that I see how happy this has made Kenny, though, I am filled with hope."

"See, Mom? This really is a good thing."

"Why do all the kids these days have children before they get married?" Belinda sounded puzzled.

"Honey," Dale said without disguising his distaste, "Kenny and Tianna are happy about this."

Tianna might have pointed out that she would not actually consider herself happy, but not wanting to spark any more awkwardness, nodded along with Kenny.

"Well, then I guess we're happy, too," Belinda said, as though trying it on for size.

"It's okay to take some time getting used to this. I know I have been surprising you a lot lately, but this one's special. Once that baby comes, I'm going to be a dad forever." Kenny radiated with glee.

Perhaps some of his mood finally rubbed off. "Well, I did see the cutest little Halloween costume at BabyStyle. Are you due by then?"

"November," said Tianna regretfully, though she privately decided that Belinda would not be overstepping her boundaries like that when the baby arrived if she knew what was good for her.

Donna's mother struggled only briefly with the reality that Kenny and her daughter were not secretly dating when Donna called to update her on recent events. Marlene had to accept that she was not going to get to do all the grandma things she had dreamed of doing with Belinda, though Belinda would still get to do them. She had never had anything against Cameron, though, so it was simple to reclaim him as her future son-in-law once she realized that there was nothing romantic between Donna and Kenny.

"Hey, how'd it go?" Cameron asked Donna when she hung up the phone, already comfortable back in Donna's apartment.

Donna rolled her eyes. "I think she finally understands that there is no Kenny and Donna wedding on the horizon."

"Doesn't that just suck? She has to revert to the ol' Donna and Cameron wedding scheme." Cameron's tone was light and sarcastic, not at all biting.

Donna laughed. "Yeah, I guess if she can't have Kenny, you'll do."

Cameron made a face. "Better Kenny than J-hole," he muttered, then immediately apologized. "I'm sorry; I promise it won't slip again." Looking ever so innocent, he bent his fingers into a 'scout's honor' pose.

"If I'd been with Kenny, though, I could be knocked up right now," Donna countered.

"I guess it's good you're with me, then," Cameron smiled, opening his arms.

Donna edged across the couch to climb inside his embrace. "It is good." She smiled blissfully. "It's really good."

After a tight squeeze, Cameron's hold loosened. "We'll get you there one day. Unfortunately, it will have to be legitimate, but I guess we can't have everything."

Stroking his arm absently, Donna smiled. She began to wonder how she could ever have considered that this was not enough for her.

It was a long moment before she replied. "So, when do you think it will be?"

Cameron frowned. "I don't know. I know I'm not ready now, and I would like to be making more money first, but I'm sure we could handle it if it came along."

"Hey, if Kenny and Tianna can do it, so can we," Donna started abruptly. "Ideally, though, I agree with you. I want to be making more money, and I feel like I still need at least a couple more years of selfishness. I want to be able to go buy $90 jeans on a whim, and things like that."

"Well, in my ideal scenario, you aren't working, so you can stay home with the baby, but that's still a few years away."

Donna snuggled in closer. "I feel so taken care of by you."

"That's the whole purpose of my life," Cameron admitted freely.

As Donna lay there with him, she questioned how she could have found this so difficult a couple weeks ago. It was like learning to use contacts, she thought. It was hard to relax her eyes enough to get used to putting the lenses in at first, and once in, they still stung for a while. After giving up on them for a few weeks, however, when she went back to try them again, she got them each in on the first try, as though she had been doing it for years. They felt comfortable and effortless, and gave her the ability to see things clearly.

"I'm so glad we're getting married," she chimed, turning to look in his eyes.

Cameron was surprised by her fervor, but his smile was genuine. "Me, too."

"I mean it. I still don't feel like I have properly apologized or that it's possible to do so."

"Honey, don't sound so dire. It's not necessary." He attempted to stroke her hair, but she pulled away.

"It is important to me. I was supposed to be looking for my dress one night when I was at *his* house, and I just felt so out of place." She looked puzzled for a moment.

"That's because you were out of place. I think you always knew that. I know I did, no matter how afraid I was that you wouldn't realize it."

Donna's face crinkled with emotion, but she did not cry. Like the lust she shared with Cameron, acceptance and forgiveness had once been so hard to imagine. So much of her life had been spent certain she would never have romantic love or the gifts that came along with it. It had been hard to trust the authenticity of it in the beginning, but again the traits surfaced, and there was no trick: it was true.

"I'm gonna use the computer for a bit to check out some more wedding ideas, if you don't mind," Donna said when she was at last secure enough to leave Cameron's side.

"Of course. Go ahead—show me if you like anything."

Donna got up, elated, wishing she did not still have more than half a year to wait for their big day, but glad she had not been presumptuous enough to forfeit their date. It was not fair, she thought, that Kenny would have his baby first.

Kenny and Tianna had not been foolish enough to start dating or living together, but they had been wise enough to become friends. As promised, Kenny visited her often and brought her whatever she needed, even if the request seemed trite. He treated her like a queen the entire duration of the pregnancy, not just when it was tough. Now they were together in the examination room of her doctor's office, waiting to learn the sex of the baby.

"I can't believe we're doing this. Twenty-one weeks." Kenny could hardly contain his enthusiasm.

"I wish I could just stay in this stage. In the beginning, I felt sick all the time, and now that I am not feeling so bad, I know that it's not long before the baby gets active." Tianna took in Kenny's ebullient look. "I know you're really into all this stuff, and you think it's totally fascinating, but you're not the one who's gotta be kicked, and have her organs squished and everything." She cringed. "Birth is so primitive. I can't believe we still have to do it naturally. I say test tube is the way to go."

Kenny laughed. "Shut up, Tia. You know you're glowing."

Tianna kept her stern expression, but felt lighter inside.

Kenny was beginning to understand her better. Disappointment was Tianna's defense mechanism for not actually being disappointed. He knew now how insecurities caused her to seek extreme closeness before she let down her guard. It was obvious in the way she acted with her family versus the way she had acted upon first meeting Kenny's own family. Only someone who knew her well could see through the feigned emotions to the real ones, and she respected those who called her on the false ones.

He had not been lying when he said that she was glowing. For the last month, especially, she seemed to emanate sunshine.

Kenny's happiness made Tianna nervous.

"Where is that stupid doctor?" she groaned, looking around as though she could see the doctor approaching through the solid wood door.

"Just relax; it's only been two minutes."

"I don't know why it always takes so long," she grumbled as the door was pushed open.

"Hello, you two." The doctor beamed merrily, though Kenny was sure she must have heard Tianna's comment. "Are you guys excited? Hopefully, we'll be able to see the sex of the baby."

Kenny nodded fervidly, but Tianna turned her nose up as if she could care less either way.

"Well, at least one of you is eager to know, so let's get to it." The doctor had not been fooled by Tianna's apparent disinterest.

When the ultrasound was underway, Tianna's exhilaration began to leak out, until she finally just let herself feel. When they learned that they would be having a girl, Tianna let out a shriek and clapped and kissed Kenny, who had been leaning over her to look at the image. Though Kenny was ready to celebrate, too, the kiss caught him so off guard that he had had a hard time keeping his head. He gave Tianna a warm look. Tianna looked shocked at her actions, but was relieved by his response.

Knowing looks ensued as they passed through the building on their way out, but by the time they were getting into Kenny's car, they were so into speculations about their little girl that a discussion of the kiss no longer seemed necessary. They were just happy to be going through it all together.

Kenny was showing Donna pictures on his cell phone of Tianna with her pregnant bulge accentuated at coffee one afternoon several weeks later.

"Wow, she's actually smiling." Donna sounded surprised. She always pictured Tianna with a scowl.

"Tia's been doing a lot more of that lately," Kenny said optimistically.

Donna looked impressed. "Tia?"

Kenny blushed.

Looking down at the last photo again, Donna groaned. "It's so unfair. When I get pregnant, I'm gonna be the fat and pissed-off type with red skin and all kinds of extra hair in odd places. Pregnancy makes Tianna look saintly."

"Nonsense. You'll glow, too," Kenny assured her. "Tianna did not even want the baby, at first, and now she lets slip how excited she is on an almost daily basis."

Donna looked dubious. She bet Tianna did not even look pregnant from behind. She had kept her tiny frame, but had the cute belly to show off. *I bet I already have more cellulite and stretch marks than she'll have when it's over*, she thought.

"Any thoughts on when that might be, by the way?" Kenny asked. "I'd always imagined our kids would be raised together."

The statement surprised Donna. "You always saw yourself with kids?"

"Well, for a long time I thought my children would have to be adopted, but yes, I did always think I would have them."

Again, Donna was impressed. "I hadn't given much thought to it until I knew of Tianna's pregnancy. I mean, I'm sad they won't be exactly the same age, but hopefully they'll be close enough to be friends, or maybe by the time I have my first, you guys will be on your second or third."

"Hey, now."

"I'm just saying..." Donna said defensively. "You seem different lately, like perhaps you're into more than just becoming a father."

"Donna, I wouldn't get your hopes up for Tianna and me to fully reconcile, let alone build a family. It's been enough of a challenge just to be friends, and much of the time she is so guarded that our friendship feels artificial."

"Well, a lot has already changed, maybe when the baby comes, it'll just happen naturally."

"We'll see," Kenny said. He did not want to jinx his chances, not even sure that they existed.

"Should I be making her a bridesmaid?" Donna asked, as though she did not want the answer to be 'yes.'

"Your bridesmaids should be people you choose for your own reasons," Kenny equivocated.

"Don't play neutral; I need to know. You are going to be a groomsman, and you have been telling me how much better you guys are getting along—do you think I should include her? She might not even accept if I asked her."

Kenny did not know what to say. "I thought I was walking with your cousin, Lahna. Wouldn't the ratio be thrown off by including her?"

Donna shrugged. "We could always have Sean, as the best man, go separately, and then have you and my brother walk with two girls each."

Kenny's feelings on the matter began to change. It wasn't that Donna wanted to get close to Tianna; it was something she wanted to do to be nice to him—a sign of acceptance of his new life. "I just don't want to be the one to tell her she'll need to fit into a nice dress two months after giving birth."

Donna was a little overeager when she said, "I'll handle it."

"Your cousins wouldn't mind?" Kenny asked just to make sure.

"I don't think they really care. The truth is, I don't have any girlfriends any more, and I've never had sisters, so I asked them and my brother's girlfriend. I thought about asking my old roommates from college, as I still think of them fondly, but we haven't even communicated in the last five years." She shrugged. "Plus, with Cameron's recent decline in male friends, we had to rearrange things, anyway."

Kenny nodded. "Then, yeah, I guess that would be nice. I'm sure she'll fuss at first, but talk past her fit, and she'll probably be extremely flattered." Kenny privately thought that he had just sounded a little like Tony when he had once tried to explain Tianna's moods to him.

"I'll put her number in my phone." Without bothering to ask permission, she lifted Kenny's phone off the table and began pressing buttons until she got to the address book. As she transferred the number into her phone, she said, "I can't believe I'm actually going to call her. It seems so weird."

"The stranger things get for me, the more normal I seem to feel," Kenny pondered aloud.

Donna looked thoughtful. "Well, to hear you tell it, you were living a lie most of your life, and now you are being your true self; I can only imagine it would feel normal."

Kenny was pensive. "What a way to put it."

"I'm the opposite. When things were weird for me, I couldn't handle it, went a little nuts, and then came back to my senses. You seem to find sense in having your life rocked a little."

Kenny smiled. "One thing we always have as a constant, though, is each other. That never wavers."

"No, it doesn't," Donna agreed somewhat absently as she looked over the menu above the order counter. Dissatisfied with her options, she faced Kenny and asked, "Do you think we should start going back to the tea and coffee place? I think I'm actually developing a taste for the vanilla tea latte again."

Kenny shook his head. Her obsession with whether or not she enjoyed the beverage would haunt him for many months, if not years, to come.

Donna had difficulty working up the nerve to call Tianna. She had not forgotten how sour things had gone in the past, and did not want to cause Kenny any grief. That being the case, she decided that going to her at Loria would be the best way to ask, especially with Cameron for support, Tony for mediation, and fresh eggplant for indulgence.

Though Cameron was willing to be dragged along, he had not fully understood the importance of including Tianna in their festivities. He assumed it was some kind of gesture between women, but as it was meaningful Donna, he was willing to go down to Loria to help.

At the host station, Donna asked for Tianna and took a seat by Cameron as they waited for her to come out. In person, she looked even more sensational, her tummy preceding her as she walked up to the front. She gave Donna a look of recognition, but it was not nearly as unflattering as the one she had given her before.

"Hello. Did you come for lunch?" she asked, bright-eyed, extending her hand for Donna to shake.

"Sort of. I mean, secondarily," Donna stuttered.

Tianna looked inquisitive.

"I was actually hoping that you had a minute to discuss something."

Tianna's eyebrows rose up another increment. "You want to discuss…?" She looked a little wary.

Donna nodded, not really wanting to delve into it at the front of the restaurant, in case it did not go well.

Tianna looked back to the gallery. There were only a few viewers, and none of them appeared to be seeking an attendant. "Okay. Shall we sit?" She gestured toward the dining room.

Donna and Cameron followed her to a table. Donna still felt awkward about asking, but there was no backing out of it now. She cleared her throat. "I'm sure you remember that Cameron and I are getting married in a few months; Kenny is one of the groomsmen." Tianna seemed with her so far. "I thought maybe you would like to be a bridesmaid? I already asked Kenny if he thought I could ask you."

Tianna looked stunned. She had expected Donna to have something to say about her relationship with Kenny, perhaps how she should marry him or maybe even how she should leave him alone after the baby comes. "You don't have to ask me just because Kenny's in it."

"No," Donna protested. "Whatever happens between you and Kenny, you are about to have a child together. You will always be part of his life, and that makes you part of my life. I hope to be very close to your daughter, and to have our children be close to each other, and I just think it would be nice if we were all included in the important events of each others' lives."

Tianna could hardly believe Donna was actually reaching out to her. She did not know if it was the pregnancy hormones, but she was so touched, she almost cried. With a hand over her heart, she accepted. "I think it would be nice, too."

Donna had been so relieved to have her question over with she had not paid much attention to the answer, and it took a moment to register. "You do?"

Cameron was beginning to feel like he could use another guy around. When Donna turned to him, he smiled, though, and appreciated how deeply she felt about the situation.

"I don't want you to worry about getting fitted for the dress; you will have plenty of time to order one after the baby comes," Donna assured her.

Tianna waved the idea away. "If am as much like my mother as my father always tells me I am, I will be back to my normal size just a few weeks after the baby comes."

"Right," Donna said, feeling that she had imposed. "Well, now that that's settled, I guess I have to add you to my list for the bridal shower. Say, what about you? Are you having a shower?"

Tianna looked down, rubbing her belly surreptitiously. "I seem to know all men."

Donna knew the feeling. "Well, not any more. Maybe you would let me throw a little one for you and Kenny. We can do the modern mom and dad-to-be type, so the guys will enjoy it, too."

Cameron wanted to hide. If Tianna said yes, he would have a role in the preparation and participation.

"You would do that?"

Donna shrugged, smiling merrily. "Of course. Everyone should have a shower."

Tianna seemed to be thinking of something, then she snapped her fingers and called for the waiter, Vinny, to come to their table.

"Go get Tony," she commanded.

Vinny did as asked, and Tony was out to them in a matter of minutes.

"Hey, it's the eggplant lover!" he called as he strode over to the table, arms out as if hugging them from several yards away. "What can I make for you today?"

"We're not ordering," Tianna corrected him. "I wanted you to come out so I could tell you something."

Tony was surprised, but his smile did not falter. "What's that?"

"I know Kenny should probably be here for this, but the timing is just too right. Tony, Donna," she looked at each in turn, "will you be our little girl's godparents?"

Donna was too stunned to speak, but Tony jumped for joy. "Aw, Tia!" He made her stand up for a hug and patted her belly delicately with the hand he just taken hers in to kiss.

Cameron looked at Donna, as shocked as she was.

"Wow! Are you sure that's what Kenny wants?" Donna felt short of breath.

Tianna nodded. "We actually had already discussed it, and had each decided on one person to ask. We were going to wait until the birth, but with both of you here, I could not pass up the opportunity."

Donna hoped her astonishment was not inconsiderate. If Kenny had asked, she would not have been so taken aback, but the fact that Tianna had done it of her own will really spoke to her. "I gladly accept."

"Hey, now that you're family, lunch is on me," Tony beamed, placing a firm hand on Donna's shoulder.

"This could be a tasty union," Donna commented, and everyone laughed.

It had apparently been a good decision to ask Tianna in person. Before that conversation, Donna could not imagine genuinely enjoying her company. She thought now that maybe Tianna was deserving of all the regard Kenny had developed for her of late. Maybe knowing the baby was coming had had just as much of an impact on her as it had had on him.

Cameron was surprised by their good fortune, even if it had committed him to a baby shower. However, now that Donna was to be godmother, it seemed a little more fitting.

As kids, Donna often forced Kenny to play MASH, which was fun until the column headings became more advanced and included topics not pertinent to the futures of males. He could do the name of the person he would marry, in what type of dwelling they would reside, what type of car they would drive, and things like that, but Donna's list eventually included specific wedding details that would not apply to him. For instance, she had wedding dress style (halter, strapless, long-sleeved), wedding dress color (white, gold, hunter green), type of bouquet (roses, irises, weeds), type of place in which to get married (church, hotel, alley), color of limo that would take them away (white, black, fuchsia with orange polka-dots), etc. She never grew tired of the endless possibilities—even when they played over the phone.

MASH

color
~~white~~
~~gold~~
h. green

style
~~halter~~
~~strapless~~
~~long sleeves~~

place
(church)
~~hotel~~
~~alley~~

bouquet
~~roses~~
(irises)
~~tulips~~

limo
~~white~~
(black)
~~fuchsia~~ ~~purple~~ ~~orange~~ ? d s

(DD+TM)

KENNY is BORED!
!!!!!

9

Donna had such a good time planning and hostessing the baby shower that thoughts of a baby of her own began to pop up more frequently and realistically than ever. Anything that could change Tianna's outlook so drastically must be amazing to experience. Donna was really coming around to the idea of being a mother, but common sense generally stepped in and reminded her of the expense, the time, and the energy it would take to raise a baby. There was also the worry about the toll pregnancy would take on her figure. She had worked so hard to achieve and maintain her current size, and she was not ready to revert to her previous state. She still needed time with her improved self-confidence before embarking upon a situation that could destroy it. She would forfeit those aspects sooner rather than later, though, she knew.

Kenny, though never wavering in his enthusiasm for the day his daughter would come, was nervous in the final weeks of Tianna's pregnancy. She was noticeably flustered by his constant fussing, and wished he would let her be. The most irritating thing had been his insistence that they join an antenatal class, but Tianna refused to add it to their breathing classes and everything else they had been doing to get ready for the baby.

Kenny had moved his computer room to the dining area of his apartment and transformed his second bedroom into a Hello Kitty nursery. He felt a little odd at first, having the baby's room at his apartment instead of at home with Tianna, but as she was still willing to let Kenny raise her, it made sense that the nursery be there. Plus, Tianna was going to stay with Kenny throughout her maternity leave so she could recover and tend to the baby. He was giving up his room completely and sleeping in the living room until she was ready to go home.

With all the preparations in place, all Kenny could do was wait. He hated that Tianna had rejected his idea that she move in with him now, before the baby was born, so she could get used to it and he could be there for anything that might happen, or she might need. Already feeling claustrophobic, Tianna had vetoed it and only agreed to move in afterwards because it was necessary to feed and care for the baby. She had been on edge for the two weeks leading up to her due date, and it may have been better for their relationship not to move in early. Kenny took solace in the fact that Tony and Stefano would both be around for her at all times.

When Kenny received the call from Tony one Tuesday morning at work, he packed up immediately, leaving to cheers from his co-workers.

"It's time for the little bambina!" Tony had announced vivaciously.

Kenny met them at the hospital and could not describe the beauty he saw in Tianna, though she was clearly not feeling it. He stayed with her while she had her check up, having Tony call Donna and his parents for him.

Tianna, with all of her natural charm, did her best to mask her fear, though Kenny consoled her, holding her hand when she had pain and brushing her long, wavy hair away from her neck and face.

After an hour, Kenny left the room briefly to update their company in the waiting area.

His mother practically dove on him, covering him in kisses, but once he could push her away, he took a breath, and collected himself. "Tianna's doing well; she's almost ready, so I just wanted to come out here and see everyone while I still could. I'm glad the whole family is here, and I hope you all get acquainted while you wait." He then introduced his parents to Tony and Stefano.

"I hope it's not too odd, considering that Tia and I are not marrying, but we will still see a lot of each other."

153

"Is Donna on her way?" Belinda asked, feeling that they could not really consider it "the whole family" until she arrived.

"It's not really her style to impose on family matters. I wouldn't expect her until after the baby is born."

Tony nodded. He had gotten the same feeling from her when he reported that Tianna was going into labor.

"But, she's the godmother." Belinda sounded let down.

"I know; she'll be here soon enough."

Belinda looked as though she had expected better manners from Donna. She unzipped her purse and dug out her phone.

"Mom, don't call her," Kenny warned, implying that it was the last thing he needed.

"I'm calling her mother," Belinda shot back defiantly. "I want to tell Marlene the happy news."

Kenny did not entirely trust her, but let it go. He turned to Dale, whose pride in his son illuminated his features. They shook hands as never before.

"Congratulations, Ken. I can't wait to meet her," he said with quiet delight.

Kenny smiled at him for a moment, and then turned to go back to Tianna. She looked even more fearful than she had when he left.

"Don't leave again," she whimpered, crying.

Kenny immediately went to coddle her. She let out a huge cry of pain, and got as close to him as possible as the spasm gradually released. He did not leave again until it was time to alert the nurse.

When the birth was over, and Mother was cradling baby with Dad at her side, Kenny felt a love he had never expected. Even through all the anticipation, the elation of the actual moment had been unpredictable. He took a few steps away to look at them together, his heart floating in his chest.

Kenny held his baby for the first time and knew her name.

"Mia," he said, peering down at her.

Tianna looked confused. "Mia?"

"That's her name," Kenny said, as though it was fact. "Mia Loria George."

"We've never discussed *Mia*. I thought we were leaning toward *Ania*." She could not understand how he could make such a capricious decision.

Kenny was not willing to discuss it. "No. She's Mia."

"You can't just name her."

"You're giving her to me; what do you care?"

"Excuse me? Whatever happened to being in each other's lives forever?"

Kenny did not care if it was selfish. When he looked at his baby's face and stroked her soft skin, he knew she was his. *You're mine, and she can't have you.*

"Kenny, give her back," Tianna demanded, putting her arms up to take her.

Kenny turned his back toward her.

"Kenny!"

"Just let me have her another minute," he squeaked, turning his head toward her.

Tianna was indignant. She had just gone through labor, and her own baby's father, who had been adulating her throughout her entire pregnancy, was now refusing to let her hold their baby. She felt deeply deceived.

Finally, after cooing to her for several long minutes, Kenny faced Tianna and handed Mia back to her.

"Thank you," she snipped unappreciatively. "Go get everyone so they can come see her," she ordered, still uncomfortable with how he had acted.

Kenny wanted to show off his little bundle of joy, but he had mixed feelings about letting anyone else too near her. When he walked out to greet everyone, Donna and Cameron were there.

"Hey, you came," he said as he reached for Donna.

"Of course." Donna smiled big. "What good is a birth without a fairy godmother?"

Kenny laughed. Cameron shook his hand and congratulated him. "She's beautiful, you guys," he crooned. "Come on back with me and see her."

Stefano bounded into the room first. He could not believe how much Tianna looked like her mother holding her when she was first born..

"Oh, Tianna, what a beautiful girl; she will be just like you!"

Donna inwardly hoped the child would only inherit Tianna's physical attributes.

As Stefano leaned in to his daughter, Kenny watched intently.

Only Donna noticed how tense it made him. "Kenny, it's okay. Stefano's not going to break her." She laughed a little, but kept her voice down. She had never known Kenny had an overprotective side.

Kenny paid no attention, though. He was focused on Stefano, who was rocking the baby too roughly for his tastes. "He's gonna drop her. She's so tiny; she'll fall right out of his arms."

Donna rolled her eyes, but did not want to make a scene.

Finally, Kenny could not take it anymore, and he hurried over and took his Mia into his own hands. *No one else can have you*, he thought.

Stefano looked a little surprised, but knew Kenny was just eager to hold her. "Have you chosen a name yet?" he asked to hide the awkwardness.

"Mia." Kenny fawned over the baby as he pronounced it.

Tianna cleared her throat meaningfully. "Actually, we haven't decided yet. *Mia* is Kenny's favorite, but I have had my heart set on *Ania*."

"*Ania* is good—a nice Italian name," Stefano concurred.

"*Mia* is very pretty," Kenny's mom interjected as though defending her son automatically, though she did not have much conviction in her statement.

Donna felt a little strange. Could she really be taking Tianna's side? Kenny was acting very peculiar.

"We'll just have to see what we agree on," Tianna stated. "I don't hate *Mia*, but I do favor *Ania*."

"Do you mind if I hold her?" Tony asked. He had actually hoped to be next after his father.

Kenny seemed a little chary of him, but handed her cautiously over.

"Hi, Mia or Ania, it's your Uncle Tony," he said in a silly baby voice. "Your godfather," he went on, tickling her tummy, marveling at her. He moved slowly toward Donna. "This is your godmother, Donna—isn't she beautiful, just like you?"

Donna blushed, but admired the baby from Tony's arms, too nervous to take her into her own. Cameron took a good peek at her, too, smiling. Tony finally brought the baby over to her other grandparents and handed her off to Belinda.

Kenny looked like an overzealous coach on the sidelines as he observed the pass.

"Kenny, quit fretting, I know how to hold a baby. I held you a billion times and never dropped you," she said, though she was concentrating on the baby rather than him.

"That was over twenty years ago," Kenny retorted lamely.

"Guess what, Kenny? The ancient techniques still work," Dale informed him as he stroked the baby's smooth skin.

When Dale had taken the baby into his arms, Belinda took a last look at her precious granddaughter and then went to her son. Throwing her arms around him, she said, "Kenny, none of us are going to hurt the baby. She'll be okay. Besides, as cute as she is right now, in two weeks, you'll sell your soul for an evening without her."

Kenny finally let his guard down a little. "I guess you're right," he admitted, though he only felt slightly more trusting.

Dale walked the baby back toward Donna. "Are you sure you don't want to hold her? It's really magical."

Donna nodded.

"Cameron?"

Cameron also declined.

"You know what? Why don't you guys spend some time together? Cam and I will wait out in the lobby. Kenny, would you mind coming out for a few minutes when you get the chance?"

Kenny nodded, and the couple excused themselves.

In the waiting area, Cameron could tell that Donna had been touched by the experience of meeting the baby. "What are you thinking about?"

Donna shrugged. "I don't know. I guess it's just weird that I am somebody's godmother. That means I get to give her presents on holidays and birthdays, take her shopping when she gets older, let her wear make-up before her parents do, take her to R movies when she's a preteen—"

The look on Donna's face scared him a little. "You don't want to expedite our plans, do you?"

"No," she laughed. "I think 'godmother' is a good compromise. I get to do all the fun stuff without even as much responsibility as an aunt."

Cameron felt a little relieved. "Phew."

Smiling, Donna turned to him. "She was really beautiful, though, wasn't she?"

Cameron nodded, smiling back.

"She'll probably be crying incessantly all night, though. Poor Tianna has to start breastfeeding." Donna grimaced. "That's enough of a deterrent for me."

Cameron laughed at her squeamishness.

"Maybe we could get a rabbit, though. We could decide to name her *Ania*, and then at the last minute, you could change her name to *Mia*," Donna joked.

"Did you think that was a little weird, too?" Cameron asked hesitantly.

"Definitely. I've never seen Kenny act like that before. It was as though he didn't want anyone else to have any say in her life." Donna clammed up when she saw Kenny approaching.

"I'm glad you got to see her," Kenny said, sounding more like himself.

"Me, too. Kenny, she's gorgeous. I can't wait to see her in her little Hello Kitty crib," Donna simpered. "I haven't been able to picture you changing a diaper yet, though. I'll have to see that one for myself."

"I am a little nervous about the first few days, but I'm sure it will be awesome once we get a rhythm going."

"Are you worried about Tianna moving in?"

"Not at all. I think it will be great for both us. Once I go back to work, she'll have the place to herself all day, and when I get home at night, I can relieve her."

Donna thought he was being idealistic. "Well, kiddo, I really am happy for you, and you should probably go back in there, so let's say goodbye, but invite me over when you are up for it."

"Thanks. I'll definitely need someone sane to talk to about everything—my mom is going to come over in the afternoons this week to help us out—we'll have to hit a happy hour or something."

Donna laughed and got ready to go. Kenny saw them onto the elevator before returning to Tianna's room.

Kenny found the first few days with Mia hectic, but rewarding. He also realized how much he had to learn from his mother. Once Kenny went back to work and Tianna was home with Mia—Kenny had won that argument despite the "Tia and Mia" disincentive—things began to get awkward. Now that Kenny and Tianna were not fully concentrated on the baby, they were confused. Neither seemed to know how s/he should act, and neither seemed to be willing to let the other in on his or her feelings.

Kenny's possessiveness regarding Mia was resurfacing, and Tianna often felt he only wanted her around because she had to feed the baby and be Mia's maternal influence. He seemed to doubt her ability to care for Mia, double-checking everything she did, and giving her the cold shoulder any time he had Mia in his arms. When she finally confronted him, he insisted he was doing nothing but caring for *his* daughter.

Until Mia was born, it had seemed Kenny and Tianna had a chance of a future together. Kenny's glee had warmed Tianna's cold heart and brought the two of them closer. Now that Kenny was playing games, Tianna seemed to be giving up on him, little slips at a time.

One day, Tianna sat down on the couch by Kenny after putting the baby down to sleep. Taking the ends of her hair between her fingers, looking dissatisfied, she commented. "I'm so glad to be able to dye my hair again. My ends are still caramel blonde, but my roots are so dark."

Kenny looked shocked. "You have to wait until you're done breastfeeding."

Tianna felt like her father had just yelled at her. "No, I don't. You're being paranoid. It's really just a precaution during the first trimester, though I waited through the whole pregnancy; it doesn't even have any proven effects on the child."

"So, you just want to chance it?"

"No! There's nothing wrong with it now, and there probably wasn't anything wrong with it before. If it'll make you happy, I'll just do highlights; the dye does not adhere to the scalp when you do highlights."

"This is just like you. You don't care about Mia. She's just an inconvenience to you."

"Kenny, I'm tired of the way you treat me. You make me feel less than human."

Kenny shrugged haughtily, not denying the accusation.

Tianna shrieked with frustration. "I don't get you lately. You treated me like a queen, and now I feel like a servant. I thought we were supposed to be getting along now. I know I've been horrible in the past, but I thought we had mended that and were moving on."

"Get real. I'm just the fag who somehow got you pregnant. You didn't even want Mia, and now that I have her, you're jealous," Kenny snapped.

Tianna sighed deeply. "It's not that I didn't want her. I was scared, and I had no idea you would be so into her. Once you reassured me we could do this, I believed you—I believed *in* you— and, now you are making me reassume all of my old doubts." She spoke calmly and sincerely, hoping Kenny would reciprocate.

Kenny turned his back to her.

After a long moment, Tianna spoke again. "Okay, if that's how it's going to be, as soon as I am back to work, we'll have to figure out custody. I may not have been ready for her, but I love her, and I will fight to maintain my rights as her mother."

Still facing away, Kenny glared with rage.

"I'm supposed to try on the dress for Donna's wedding at the end of this week, but I'll call her and tell her to forget having me there. She wanted to celebrate with the important people in her life, and I was only important by association. You go and have fun. I'll watch Mia."

Even though he could not see her face, Kenny knew that she was about to cry, no matter how brave she tried to sound.

"You should go. Donna's the godmother of your child, isn't she?" he said with more kindness than he had used in days.

"No. She's the godmother of *your* daughter," Tianna stated without bitterness, but with a huge disappointment. "I'm just indirectly associated."

Sadness was evident in her tone, accompanied by despair and betrayal. It was so honest it finally turned Kenny back into a reasonable adult.

Tianna was looking away this time.

"Hey," Kenny began as pleasantly as he could. She flinched at the hand he had placed on her shoulder. "Tianna, I'm sorry. I never imagined that I would feel this way, and I certainly never imagined that I would treat you so poorly."

A glimmer of hope raced through her heart, but it only made tears more likely to come.

"I know I haven't treated you like an equal; I just now realized it's because I haven't thought of you as one. I *have* been thinking of you as a resource for Mia and treating you no better." The guilt he felt was observable in his posture.

Tianna tried to hide her sniffles, but it was impossible now that she was face to face with him. He smiled weakly, brushing the tears from under one eye with his thumb. She did not struggle against him this time, but she was unable to stop the crying. Kenny broke down and put his arms around her, apologizing profusely as he tried to hold in his own tears. After a long moment, Mia started crying, too, and they pulled away from each other, laughing.

Tianna looked uncertain; her instinct was to go to her child. Kenny gave her a reassuring boost of confidence, and she went to Mia, feeling the joy of family for the first time. Kenny trailed in a little after, giving Tianna a few minutes of privacy with Mia. He watched her handle Mia in a whole new light than he had before, and began to feel the familiar awe of her that he had felt when she was pregnant, and realized for the first time that it was love.

"You know, it's not too late to change her name. We did leave it undecided on the birth certificate."

Tianna smiled, turning to look awkwardly over her shoulder at him, so that Mia would face him directly as she bounced her. "No. We don't have to do that."

"Are you sure? We really had decided to go with *Ania*, and I just barged in with *Mia*."

Tianna laughed. "You know what? It's actually grown on me. I like looking at her, and thinking she's *Mia*."

"What does your father think, though?"

"Are you kidding? He loves it. The whole Italian thing is just a front; besides, *Mia* can be traced back to many European origins."

They shared a nice laugh, enjoying their time with the baby before placing her back in the crib.

"I don't want to spoil this moment because I think it's the truest one we've ever shared, but I want to say something else about my behavior," Kenny admitted as they tiptoed out of the nursery.

Tianna was a little unnerved by the gravity of his tone, but did not attempt to stop him.

"After we broke up, I went to Tucson to confirm the news of Marcos' passing."

Tianna looked up, startled, but did not interrupt.

"As it turned out, he did have AIDS, and he did die from it."

Tianna's hand flew across her mouth. Her eyes began streaming as she shook her head in disbelief.

"Even though I hadn't had contact with Marcos that would put me in jeopardy of contracting the disease, I took a test before I left Tucson, just to make sure. I want you to know that even though I hated you then, I would have told you if there was any possibility you could be in danger." Kenny had to look away to keep himself from crying.

"You should hate me. I'm a terrible, awful person. I may not understand that lifestyle, but I never should have said those things. I believe I was jealous. I mean, against another woman I could have competed, but there was no way I could have rivaled a guy, and I could not bear the thought of losing you to one."

Kenny smiled at her. "I guess I never thought of it like that, but you are not a terrible, awful person. Maybe in that moment you were, but now that moment is over, and you are a kind and loving mom who has become almost complacent to my foolish little demands. Lately, I've been the one that hasn't deserved you."

Tianna laughed, but only at how emotional they had each been since Mia had been born. "How about we both just knock it off? People always say how crazy you get when you are taking care of your first baby, but I didn't think it would go this far."

"I agree. Let's remember how it was in there a few minutes ago, when everything was perfect, and know that it never needs to be any different."

Tianna moved into Kenny's outstretched arms and held him the way she could not remember doing even at the beginning of their relationship. She felt like she loved Kenny, and he loved her back, and there would be no more denial from either party.

Donna was never told of how close Tianna came to revoking her acceptance of her role as bridesmaid. When she arrived at their apartment that Friday after work to see Mia before taking Tianna to try on the dress, everything between them seemed to be as good as it had been by the end of the pregnancy.

After playing with Mia a little while, reminding her every few lines that she was her godmother, she noticed how well the couple interacted. Though she knew it was an odd comparison, she especially noticed how comfortable Kenny had become around Tianna—very much as he had always been with Marcos.

"You guys are doing such a great job," Donna finally marveled. "I mean, the house is clean, and you seem to have all of Mia's things right when and where she needs them."

Kenny laughed, though he was proud to hear it. "Well, what'd you think—we'd move into a trailer, with Mia sleeping in the kitchen sink?"

"No!" Donna felt herself flush. "I just mean you seem so together. I can just imagine the fright my house would be in if I was in your position. I think I would be bawling to Cameron every time he came home. There would be dishes piled up and baby toys all over the living room. I mean, the way I keep house now would probably be considered child endangerment."

The couple laughed, but shared a secret knowledge of how appearances could be deceiving.

"Well, it really helps being home with her all day," Tianna insisted shyly.

Donna still thought they deserved credit. Though she could never have thought it almost a year prior, she was glad they had been brought back together.

At the dress shop, Donna could not believe how Tianna had kept her figure. In fact, if anything was different, it was a little enlargement of the chest.

"See, what'd I tell you?" Tianna said as she presented herself to Donna and the tailor, stepping out to the main mirror after getting into the dress. "Just like my mother."

Tianna was wearing a rich, red satin gown with sash and gloves to match. She played with the arrangement of her hair in front of the mirror. "I can't wait to have my hair done again," she smiled, feeling very sentimental as she said it, but keeping the reason secret, not wanting to place any undue stress upon Donna.

"You can wear it how you like," Donna informed her. "The only requirement is that you work a little rose ornament into it somehow. I don't think I have a picture with me, but the florist attaches them to pins or combs, so you'll have to let me know which you'd prefer when it gets close to the day."

Tianna nodded. She felt so beautiful in her dress that she was beginning to get a little envious of Donna, who would be the one to wear white. "Is your gown here, too?"

"Yeah. It's being worked on, but they have another one just like it that I can show you." Donna was surprised by how much interest Tianna was taking in her and how friendly she had been. It was a complete turn-around from their first meeting.

A short while later, Tianna was dressed again and had followed Donna to the bridal salon to view her gown. When Donna pulled it off the rack, the corners of Tianna's mouth stretched further and further into smile.

"You like it that much?" Donna asked bashfully.

"I adore it!" Tianna took long strides until she was close enough to grasp the dress in her hands, examining all the fine details. "You have to put it on!"

"What? No, no. I couldn't, anyway. This one is two sizes smaller than mine."

"Oh, just do it, anyway. It won't matter if it doesn't zip up all the way; I just want to see it on you."

Donna could not refuse. "Okay."

Once Donna had it on, for the most part, she came out from behind the curtain to applause, not just from Tianna, but from a couple of other shoppers, as well.

"Wow! You look fantastic!" Tianna shouted a little more loudly than Donna liked. "Your arms especially look good— have you been working on them?"

Donna nodded.

"Maybe I should do mine, too. The gloves make the forearm look so dainty that the bare shoulder and upper arm is conspicuous." Tianna rolled up her sleeve to examine her arms as she stood beside Donna in front of the mirror.

Donna could have punched her for having such a naturally athletic build. "I think you looked great in that dress. I wouldn't change a thing."

"I think it was the first time I've ever looked busty," Tianna laughed, thrusting out her chest, still looking in the mirror.

Donna laughed, too. "There is definitely cleavage, but you're still a far cry from Pamela Anderson."

"Are you kidding? Pamela Anderson isn't even Pamela Anderson. Haven't you seen her early fitness model photos?"

Donna was laughing uncontrollably, feeling like she did in junior high, not a care in the world about the stares she got from other people. The evening seemed to confirm that she had made the right decision in asking Tianna to join in the festivities.

The day of Donna and Cameron's wedding came faster than they had known it could. The three months that had transpired since Mia's birth had zoomed by at an unexpected rate.

It was her wedding day at last, and Donna watched herself in the mirror as Tianna stuck a few more pins under her veil to keep it in place. The other bridesmaids sat on a sofa sipping champagne, ready to go, waiting for their cue to take their positions in the procession. Donna could not have imagined being there without Tianna, whom she had unexpectedly come to view as her maid of honor, though she had never officially chosen one.

"Now, it's perfect." Tianna beamed as she gently laid the front layer of the veil over Donna's face.

Donna smiled, too, as she examined herself from several angles. Tianna stepped back to allow her room to twirl her dress. In her mind, Donna heard the song that had always inspired her, and she had secretly adopted as her theme song for the day: Nina Simone's "Feelin' Good." Suddenly, Donna was alone in the room with Nina and the jazz band, and she was not an ugly little girl playing dress up, wishing she were beautiful. She was herself—a donna—long, brown hair in curls, pulled back just a tad from her face; immaculate, white, satin gown with decorative folds over the torso and just a hint of sparkle lining the edge of her veil, which caught the light with each new position she took. For once, she had nothing negative to say about herself.

There had been a few glitches in the seating arrangement and a last-minute menu substitution, but once she walked down the stairs to wait for the procession to begin, everything was perfect. The emotion of the day did not hit her until she saw her usually cantankerous dad all dressed up, waiting to take her arm, Kenny and Tianna holding Mia between them with a little basket of rose petals, which Tianna would be throwing. Her big brother looked dapper with his girlfriend on his arm, and her two cousins were all dressed up, each on one arm of Cameron's brother Sean. And, Cameron was out there, waiting for her.

She felt the emotion well up until she was light and warm. She had never felt this degree of elation before; it could never be duplicated. She was so in love that everything looked gorgeous to her, and she felt like laughing, though she did not have enough breath for it. She waited eagerly for her turn to exit to the aisle—she would later recall telling her dad how she was so happy, but not making much sense in her dither. Donna hardly noticed the audience, and though she saw many familiar faces, all she could think was of Cameron.

The look on his face when he finally saw her was of pure, exalted love. He had been very careful to take in absolutely no detail of her look for the evening prior to the event, and his discretion had paid off. The sight of her was made even more impressive by having had nothing to anticipate. Even Sean, who stood beside him, could not believe how taken he, himself, had been by her.

Their ceremony was short, followed immediately by the bride and groom picture session, which had been left until after they had seen each other, though the separate ones had been taken in advance. Throughout the photo shoot, Donna pondered how she felt about her new name. She had loved DiSimone, but thought Ellis was great, too. 'At least people will be able to spell and pronounce it," she thought as she took a moment between photos to massage her aching jaw. The only thing she found odd about the transition was that there did not seem to be much of one. Today, she woke up "Donna DiSimone," and tomorrow she would be Donna Ellis, and there was nothing strange about it. It seemed so natural, and yet she felt no loss of connection to the family with whom she had grown up.

Once Kenny, Tianna, and Mia were done with their photos, they brought Mia to sit with Tony and Stefano, who would later admit that he spent one hundred and eighty dollars on Mia's dress, while they took their seats at the head table.

"It's still hard to believe that was Donna up there," Kenny remarked dreamily.

"I thought she looked amazing in the store with her dress on, but there are no words for how she looks tonight."

Kenny was stunned by Tianna's praise. "You really mean it?"

"I do. I feel like she and I could be good friends. I mean, let's face it, neither of us seem to get along with other girls too well, though we have both found a way to laugh with each other. Plus, we are both very fond of you."

"That's really great, Tia." Kenny was sincere enough for his voice to quiver. "I must be getting caught up in all this happiness." He tried to blow it off.

Tianna put an arm around him, rubbing his shoulder. "I know. I am, too, but *this* at least is not merely a product of the moment."

Kenny's forehead wrinkled as he looked at her, not quite understanding.

Tianna removed her gloves to take Kenny's hands. Smiling, staring deeply into his eyes, she asked, "Kenny, will you be my husband?"

Kenny reeled. "What?"

"I'm serious, Kenny. I know we don't have everything figured out, but we're getting there, and I want us both to be there for Mia, too. I want her to have at least two siblings— eventually," she stressed heavily, "and I want us all to be a family."

The proposition was so unforeseen that Kenny was still trying to put it together. Was she saying that she truly wanted to get married, or just that she wanted to be married, so they could have more kids with the same genes?

She understood what he was thinking. "I don't mean just for Mia. I want *us* to be together. I don't think anyone else has ever broken me down quite the way you have—and I don't mean that in a bad way. We have each hurt each other, but we don't have to do that any more."

They had been getting along better than ever, and they did live and raise a baby together, but was marriage right for them? Kenny was about to tell her he was too uncertain to commit to an answer, but as the words came out of his mouth, "I will," is what he said.

Tianna gasped. "I can't believe it!" She bounced in her seat. "You will? You really, really will?"

Kenny was flabbergasted by her reaction. "Yes," he guaranteed, matching her ebullience.

"I can't wait to ask Donna to be my maid of honor! Of course, I'll have to wait until after her honeymoon—one person's glory at a time, right?"

Kenny could not wipe the grin off his face. Her unrestrained expression astounded and amused him.

A waiter cleared his throat on the opposite side of the table. "I think champagne is in order," he presumed in a foreign accent, smiling knowingly.

Kenny and Tianna shared an odd look.

"Don't worry, I will not tell the bride. You'll come back soon, then, yes?"

They both gave him a huge smile, and he handed each of them two glasses from his tray. "One for now, and one for later, I think."

Kenny and Tianna clinked glasses, unable to remove their eyes from each other, and drank down their toast. When they were done, they looked back to Tony, Stefano, and Mia. Stefano had her pseudo-standing on his lap, trying to get her to wave at them, and Tony was smiling at them, even from afar, able to see that they were in love.

K enny did not mention his engagement to Donna until after she and Cameron had gotten back from their honeymoon. He thought Donna looked better than ever, even though she insisted it would take her at least six weeks to lose all the weight she had gained on their seven-day cruise. Her skin was still fair, but the hint of color from the Caribbean sun and the rosy glow of being newly wed made her appear radiant.

Donna took the compliment, but forgot all about her self-image when she heard Kenny's news. It was so hard to imagine that her little gay boy had grown into a guy's guy. In hindsight, she realized it had been about a year since he told her he was living a lie and months since she had thought of him as gay. He already had a baby, and was now going for a wife—maybe even more babies—it was an enormous turn around, and yet it seemed Kenny was finally on track. Maybe he had needed to be a dad to find his niche in life, and maybe he had needed Tianna beside him to keep from becoming too obsessed with the role.

She was happy for them both. She was glad that she and Tianna had bonded a little; the two couples would be able to share so much.

"We're not going to have the big wedding you and Cameron had, but we're not eloping, either. With the baby already born, what's the point, right?" Kenny gave a shy laugh as he looked around Donna's living room, still full of tons of unopened presents.

Donna smiled lovingly at him. "You guys will have a great wedding. And maybe I'll be able to re-gift you a bunch of good stuff." She teased then, drew a dreamy breath. "Can you remember who we were two years ago?"

Kenny fell in line with her mood. "Do I have to?"

They shared a moment—both relaxed, yet not at all weighed down. They had already been sitting close to each other, but were now practically leaning on each other, heads touching, not unlike conjoined twins. To an onlooker, their bodies would form the shape of a heart, with shoulders in, hips out, and knees in.

"Can you believe that our moms thought we were dating?" Donna finally commented. "Even though it was months ago, it's still so crazy."

"I know." Kenny gave a sigh of disbelief. "How wrong they had it."

"Yeah. Not as wrong as you did, though." She jabbed at him.

"Hey. I figured it out eventually, didn't I?"

"You did," Donna conceded. "And I don't think your *gay days,*" she gave the phrase a silly emphasis, "were wasted. You had a special friend in Marcos, even if it was more platonic than you thought. He needed you to keep his spirits high."

"That's a nice way to look at it."

"Well, it's true. Plus, you probably would have been a lot less fun to grow up with if you were just another boy."

Kenny did not have to wonder where all this was coming from because he also felt it. "Donna, do you think we've actually become real people?"

"No." She sounded confident. "But we sure are a lot closer. I am still of the belief, though, that people like you and me never make it all the way to real; we become something similar, but I don't think real people necessarily understand that they are set apart. The thought to analyze the situation that way would simply not occur to them."

"Yeah, they wouldn't have the kind of time it takes to perform the sophomoric scrutiny of everyone else around them." Kenny laughed at himself.

"We're blessed enough to know it, but not enough to do anything but strive for what we know we are unlikely to achieve," Donna sighed.

"Who knows, though? You just mentioned how much we changed in only two years. Maybe we'll catch it on the next wave of progress," Kenny said hopefully.

"Maybe," Donna concurred without actually committing to it.

Printed in the United States
78875LV00002B/54